MW00573526

Woman in the Tower

Woman in the Tower

Stories for the Wounded Child

by Richard Lance Williams

Dalton Publishing
P.O. Box 242
Austin, Texas 78767
www.daltonpublishing.com

Printed in the United States of America

Edited by Robert Stikmanz

Cover art by Chris Hay

Cover design by Tamar Design+Marketing and Jason Hranicky

Interior Design and Typesetting by Deltina Hay

ISBN-13: 978-0-9817443-5-3

Library of Congress Cataloging-in-Publication Data

Williams, Richard Lance, 1952-
Woman in the tower / Richard Lance Williams.
p. cm.
ISBN 978-0-9817443-5-3
1. Fairy tales--Fiction. 2. Self-actualization (Psychology)--Fiction. 3. Conduct of life--Fiction. I. Title.
PS3623.I5595W66 2009
813'.6--dc22
2008039248

for all of the women in my life

Author's Note

This book began as an exercise for a graduate class. I wanted to write a fairy tale that hewed as close to a Grimm's fairy tale as I could, one that was absolutely devoid of modern irony. It was not easy. I resorted to using my youngest child as my primary guinea pig. Five is an age that trucks no irony.

Several rewrites later her face registered my success. Flush with that achievement, I wanted more (yes, we know). I wanted to write a human development story (a classically inflected romance) in fairy tales that also traced, more or less, the evolution of fairy tales, one that would, indeed, finally employ modern irony. (The graduate school I attended is Pacifica Graduate Institute, home of the Joseph Campbell library and archives. His famous analysis of Star Wars and the hero cycle is a marvelous template for tracking the ancient roots of modern tales.)

I employed the Aarne-Thompson tale types as a general guide for how to tell the tales, but really relied on tempered intuition, an archetypal compass far older than the academy's imprimatur. While the tales describe a character arc, they were written to stand on their own.

An early reader suggested I subtitle the work: Stories for the Wounded Child. Perhaps he was right. Still, here's to the healing child. May she and he welcome the wonders of adulthood, being, as James Hillman notes, as appropriate, childlike and not childish.

I must acknowledge the deep influences of Carl Jung (specifically his alchemical works), James Hillman (*Re-Visioning Psychology* is one of the greatest contributions to psychology in all its relatively short history), and especially Marie-Louise von Franz, whose stunningly brilliant seminal work in the Jungian interpretation of fairy tales still staggers the imagination. The remarkable fiction of Jorge Luis Borges cannot go unacknowledged nor can we fail to mention John Gardner and his *Grendel.*

Personal thanks for their early feedback and encouragement go to David Kramer, April Rossi, Kathleen Jenks (whose classes at Pacifica were the impetus for these stories), and Ramona and Kady, my scarily intelligent and beautiful daughters, who were the earliest ears to hear these tales. And lest we forget our origins, my mother Gloria and her sense of humor and my niece April for her unending kindness.

Thanks to Christy Kale-Williams for putting up with me all these years. And, of course, to Rob Lewis for his superb editorial suggestions, to Christopher Hay for his wondrous illustrations, and to Deltina Hay for her gentle but relentless encouragement to deliver a final product. What gifts they are.

Table of Contents

I had a dream, or it had me…

—Rex Rains

Beginnings

The sages tell us that every beginning is an ending, every ending a beginning. Death is a curtain. Life a stage. Death a stage. Life a curtain. Somewhere there is a place where all this is obvious. A heaven. A hell. Nirvana. Maya. The illusionless illusion. The spiraling circle. The point beyond the point that is not a point yet is the whole point.

And there is that place between.

The doorway.

The liminal.

Neither here nor there, but someplace where joy and suffering have not separated and everything depends on a choice that can't be made, that must be made.

The between place.

This is the place of myth, of fairy tale, of a sublime truthless truth. The place where all that we desire and all that confounds us plays an infinitely beguiling game of hide and seek. A grand peek-a-boo.

But if we are lucky or unlucky enough (Blessings. Curses. Which is which in the long view?) to get to this point of consciousness, if we manage through hook, crook, grace, or grab to achieve a level of intimate understanding of this strange game called human life, we are always left with further questions, questions that defy technological advance or dogmas' best interpolations. It stopped Augustine cold. Wittgenstein, too. Visionary and mathematician, both came to the same conclusion: silence and a life still to be lived.

What we do not know, what tortures us if we are tortured and what delights us if we are delighted, are the ages' old unanswerable questions:

Who is the hunted and who the pursued? What the treasure and what the cost?

Every beginning an ending, every ending a beginning.

We, arms upraised and faces questioning, always find ourselves somewhere in the middle of this path of inexorable truth, this journey that fills us alternately with dread and with wonder.

Yet, some get lucky. Some, like this Everyman, No Man, find in the dark, in the most improbable of places and the most imponderable of times, a Guide to lead us into and through the most terrifying and most beautiful of all places.

She, whose names are more numerous and whose power touches deeper in time than human tongues may speak, she who we call the dark woman in the tower, became this man's, this human's, guide into that frightening and mysterious realm of the labyrinthine heart.

* * *

Like Dante, he found himself at middle age lost in a wilderness of despair wondering where his once promising life had gone wrong. And not just his life, but everything. The music, the clothes, the art, the jobs. Everything. What had happened to the people he had once believed in? Those who spoke of beauty and art and nature, of freedom and justice and peace, who knew that faith and hope and love were not childish ideals, but truths that beyond understanding were necessary for human life?

Somewhere, somehow, they lost a connection to that remarkable promise that had been on everyone's tongue. A promise as great as any civilization had ever proposed.

Pfft. Gone. As if it were a...pipe dream. A promise written in the smoke rings from the houkah of the caterpillar in Alice's afternoon dream.

They, those children so full of visions of an embracing love that reached higher even than the sages they emulated, they spoke now of Wall Street, pensions, and worry about old age insurance plans. All ideas well and good and necessary. But their passion for the heart, their soul and spirit? Surely it wasn't a question of aging. These children were old before they began.

What happened? Was it he who missed the point?

Wisdom couldn't lie in stock dividends, could it? If it were all good, why the hell was everybody so damned worried?

He just didn't want to think about it anymore.

Alas, there were no Platos to guide him. Heroes were passé. Even if you miraculously found one, it wouldn't be long before you found out the hero had a thing for…for whatever, some stupid, ignominious trait.

It just wasn't worth the distraction.

Wisdom? Wisdom was a hackneyed concept nobody wanted to explore save with a clothes pin on their nose and a release form in their gloved hand. A claim of wisdom was tantamount to declaring a quarantine. Only the seriously desperate approached the wasteland of Wisdom.

The church? Well, the church was a second tier HMO, overpriced and bogged down with infighting and blind adherence to outdated rules and regulations.

He found himself listening to bad radio, reading unsolicited emails from psychics and channelers and even real estate schemers.

What his life had meant, and what lay in the darkness that was to become his future, were ciphered ephemera beyond his ken. He had no idea of who he was. He only knew who he no longer wanted to be. He knew he could not be what they said he had to be, nor could he be merely the dark shadow opposed to them—whoever they were. He had to become as the poets say: his own true self, no matter the slipperiness of the concept of self.

So he started walking. He'd read that walking led many a troubled man to a solution. Problems that gnawed at the mind and spirit dissolved in walks and left in the walker's life a solution at once obvious and clear. Inventions, concepts, works of art, religions: all born from the act of walking.

Walking, and then finding a spot made familiar by the repeated act of seeing it every day, and then resting. Sitting as with an old friend. Turning the simplest of acts, the most familiar of territories into a miraculous, momentous occasion. And then hearing in the silence of listening. Hearing the voice of that old friend, new words. Seeing in folds of that hill, the bending of those meadow grasses a light unlike any light he has known before.

So he walked to find a solution to the pain in his heart and soul. Not the solution, but a solution. That was more than enough to ask from putting one foot in front of the other.

Walking. Day after day. Further and further afield. Closer to the moment. Closer. But nothing changed. He could feel his resistance. He could feel his desire turn away from itself. The hills did not open. The light did not bend around the dark star of his self-pity.

But he kept walking. And one day he rose at dawn and walked all day. He walked toward the ocean some thirty miles from his home. But when he heard the ocean just beyond a low hill he stopped. Something about the ocean he could not face. But he could not stop walking. So he turned south and walked along a path that paralleled the water but kept it out of sight. He walked until the sun went down. Until a fog rolled in so thick it swallowed even the darkness. And still he walked.

It began to rain. Slow and steady and cold and he began to cry.

Still he walked. Each step heavier. On and on until each step became a knife in his legs, and then his arms, his lungs, and at last his heart. Pierced with knives he finally stopped, but he would not fall. His eyes closed. His face contorted with the pain his tears could not bear away. Swaying like a drunken giant about to teeter from his clouded castle.

"Look up."

The voice.

He opened his eyes.

He raised them. There, on top of a ridge. A light. A tower. A window and a figure pacing the floor.

"Remember."

He looked to the right and took a step and collapsed into unconsciousness.

Dust eventually settles. Forms a film, a layer, a slate, a chunk, a rock, a mountain, a chip, a speck, a mote. Dust eventually settles where the winds do not whip it toward the cold aridity of space. The rain does not drive it weeping down. The sun does not punish it. Dust eventually settles we are told. It has been pushed around enough and it burns.

He stood outside his house staring at the brass door knob as it turned from within.

He could not move. The door knob turned and turned again. His right side went numb. Who could be in there? There was not supposed to be anyone in there. The house was empty. He was outside. What was turning the door knob?

Why was he inside his house now? He hadn't moved. Yet here were the stairs. There the closet. A hand. Reaching. Huge.

He startled himself awake. A coyote stood six paces from him, head lowered, staring at him, slowly moving its head side to side.

The man screamed, shut his eyes and screamed as loudly and as high pitched as he possibly could. The coyote scrambled away with a yip and a scattering of stones.

"What am I doing?" He sat on a rocky path about midway up the side of a long, low ridge. The ocean lay green and flat a half a mile to his right. The sun was up but clouds hid it. He watched them still half asleep, still frightened. They moved so slowly, ribbons of mist, swathes of dew waiting to be slathered on stones and the tiny white mountain flowers quivering in the chill morning air. The clouds draped from the tops of the redwoods like watery serpent angels, fingers of God kneading the earth to life, wrapping around each mote of light, new skin, a silvery gleam, the liquid color of his dreams.

Smiling softly, he swayed as if he were a small white flower held in the arms of spirit air—at once at peace and beyond the need for comfort.

He took a deep breath and remembered the vision of the tower on a hill. He looked alertly to his left. Nothing. He took another deep breath. He was glad it wasn't there. He wasn't ready.

"What a fool," he said aloud.

He stood and looked around. Which way to go? He studied the path for a few seconds. Follow the coyote toward the tower or head the other way, back up the ridge.

He looked back across the valley to where the light had been.

But then again, he thought, the clouds were so thick. The sun was up. If it were there, the light would have been turned out by now so how could he expect to see it?

The shadow in the window. It was a woman's shadow. It felt young.

What time was it? No telling what time it was. Except it felt early. The quiet of dawn has its own inescapable quality, just like her shadow in the window. A young woman. Troubled. A story to tell. Worried. Just like him. There she was, wealthy enough to own a tower by the sea. Beautiful, no doubt. And pacing the floor of a tower.

Not much different than walking a darkened path like a fool in a rainstorm. Waiting for dawn's particular light, its peculiar anticipatory silence.

He scratched his head with both his hands and grimaced. So many dawns alone. He breathed into his palm and shivered.

"Maybe later," he sighed and headed back up the slope.

At the top of the ridge he stopped and studied the grey waters of the Pacific. A few surfers in black wet suits bobbed on the glass far to his right. Ever hopeful. He wished he had that kind of patience, that passion for a moment.

How many minutes of real joy are there in a life? How many minutes of suffering? The suffering so unnecessary, so anticipatory of catastrophe, not real. Real suffering rarely lasted more than a few minutes, a few hours of pure torture at the very worst and by then shock took care of most of the pain.

Even in the concentration camps—the worst horror of all—even there the suffering was mostly anticipatory. Though the anticipated horror was unspeakably real. Still, in that place….

Still, time passes regardless of your individual circumstance. Concentration camp or circus. There are moments of joy and moments of tragedy. Between those moments lies our life as lived. He didn't think those surfers faced the glass the same way he did. They saw a wave to ride, a colorful parade of pleasurable sensations. He saw a flatness that went on forever or swelled suddenly and crushed him against the insensate rocks, leaving his broken bones for scavenger sharks and the relentlessly pounding waves.

A tanker cut through the mist still clinging to the distant islands, then disappeared back into the mist, swallowed whole.

He shrugged. None of this philosophy mattered. Elucidation in the mists of his life was always transitory. He used to want to cry when that thought washed over him. Inured. That's what he'd become.

Try as he might, he was simply a man who could not wait with hope in the cold waters of his life.

Besides, he had a dreadful fear of the ocean.

A squawking seagull swooped by his head, the gull's beak combing through the middle of his hair from the forehead to the crown. The man yelped and cursed, flailing at the air as if a flock of gulls were about to devour him. He dabbed at the scratch. Blood. Not a lot. But he was cut. He squinted into the suddenly visible sun, trying to follow the course of the bird.

There, across the valley, the tower stood before him. The world fell into utter silence. Only the top half of the tower stood above the enshrouding morning fog. No light shone from the one visible window. The blackened stone seemed from an age beyond that possible for a castle in North America.

"Imported," he said aloud then hunched defensively and self-consciously looked around as if expecting a crowd to laugh at his ridiculously inappropriate response. "Something dark from afar," he whispered, trying to convince himself that he wasn't as insipid as he felt himself to be. "Something dark with a light inside. Something new to guide me into…to change this…I'm too tired for this. Oh, god, I can't even be honest with myself when I'm ready to die."

He stood with his eyes closed trying to still his mind. Thinking nothing, thinking nothing, he said silently. Nothing. Nothing. Ten seconds passed and his eyes popped open.

"Well, at least I know that I can't be honest with myself." He turned and bowed to his imaginary audience. "Enough philosophy. Time for action." He took a quarter turn, then another and two more. "The four directions," he proclaimed and stretched out his arms. "I will remember this place." He circled once more, more slowly, making a precise mental note of his location. "Okay," he shouted and clapped his hands twice. "Remembered."

He hustled back along the ridge. Two hours later he found a convenience store, called a cab, and hit the bed still in his jacket.

When he woke from his ten-hour nap he hopped on the Web and surfed up some maps of the coast.

Geography fascinated him. Map reading had intrigued him since he was old enough to know what a map was. He used to draw treasure maps on unfolded paper bags—they looked old. But the treasure wasn't pirates' gold. What he sought held greater riches than mere gold. He wanted true escape. He wanted another dimension.

He imagined there were places, small places no bigger than a clover patch, that were gateways to other worlds. They could be in a playground. Or on a median strip. Places passed by a million people, but somehow everyone had always just missed the spot. Just inches away, a half inch, a quarter inch. No one stepped on the spot just right.

And those who did were taken to another world anyway. If they came back who would believe them? The place changed. When you went through, it changed, it moved. You could take them to the place and they'd stomp around and look at you like you were an idiot and no matter how you swore, no matter how you cried, no one would believe you. After a while even you would believe it had never happened. It wouldn't even have the validity of a dream.

It was his luck to still believe that such places were real. He hoped his castle were such a place. He hoped despite his rational certainty that it wasn't, that it couldn't be, that no such place existed outside dreams and fairy tales and the mad visions of fearful priests.

He didn't believe in UFOs or any version of the prince on the horse rescuing us from the dreary desperation of our lives. He didn't believe in saviors, in heroes. And he wanted to. He wanted to so much, but he just couldn't. Yet, as he studied the maps his desire for relief from the misery of his existence grew more and more desperate: nothing seemed to match the topography he remembered. Might as well have been the coast of Ireland he'd seen.

"Ireland," he whispered, almost a curse as much as a thought. He typed the word in the search box. He stared at it. The word itself became a landscape. He could see the mystery, the ruins, the ancient loneliness. "She's from there, at least," he thought. "A place of forlorn beauty." He stared for a few minutes, lost in a self-pitying reverie, wanting to be wrapped in the diaphanous covered arms of a faery queen. Taken to the Land of the Young. A land without computers and bitter pettiness.

The phone rang. He glanced at the number. Business.

He shivered. No business. No escape into that world tonight. No, he wanted to go to the center of it. The center of the thing itself. A place where he couldn't rely on his own copingly delusional tricks.

"Self-knowledge only goes so far, doesn't it now?" he snitted peevishly at his reflection in the window. "Let's hit the darkness again."

He flicked off the computer, let the answering machine do its thing, grabbed his coat and keys, and headed in the general direction of the coast. He was going to get lost in order to find himself.

* * *

Three hours later he was parked in the middle of a forest with his headlights off and his right hand bloody.

Utterly lost and suddenly not at all happy about it, he had stormed in frustration from his car and smashed his hand into the trunk of a piñon.

He was pretty sure he'd broken at least one finger, but his anger hadn't left him and the pain had not yet become a throb.

A coyote howled to his right. Close to his right.

And then the thing was on him, pulling at the sleeve of his down jacket with a surprising fury. Feathered padding filled the air. Instinctively he started spinning, spinning and lifting the animal off the ground. The coyote let go and ran under the Jeep and out the other side. It turned and howled again before charging past him to the edge of darkness, just beyond the headlights' reach.

"What?" he offered up in his best tough guy impersonation. He should have been scared stiff, but he started to laugh. "I'm not a roadrunner, pal. I just happen to be in the middle of this desert called 'What the hell is going on with my life?' If you got something to offer, I'm ready. Okay? Just show me what you want."

The coyote sat and looked over its shoulder then back.

"You want me to wait, then follow you? What? Are you Lassie's country cousin? Come on. Show me, now. Show me."

The coyote trotted up to him, yipped and turned back around and walked four steps and stopped.

"Fine. I'm with you."

His jaw clenched tightly. This was it. He'd once had a gun held to his head in a robbery, but it was nothing; it had all happened so fast, a quick exchange of money for your life. Simple as a movie contrivance. But this? This was the most frightening thing he'd ever known. And each step brought only deeper fear. This exchange held greater danger. This was his life or his soul.

And one step followed another. He really had no other choice. This was it. The beginning. The end.

The place was utterly dark. It was a small stone cottage with a tower on its south side, a narrow porch on the east side—the front entrance. Trees bordered it close—maybe five paces from the outer walls to the trees' shadows—on the north, south, and west, though there was a clearing on the west that revealed low rolling hills running down to another spur of woods and the ocean calmly glistening beyond it. All the windows were covered with dark drapery.

The door was heavy oak, its latch a bronze lion's head.

Slowly he stepped onto the porch. A board creaked. He winced and the door opened just enough for him to see a light. Candlelight. Classic. He forced a grin to keep himself from vomiting up his belly full of fear.

A shadow passed inside the room. He jumped from the porch and ran back several feet before he tripped over the yipping coyote. It scrambled back away from him then trotted toward the cottage and disappeared into the woods to the north.

He caught his breath, then called out softly from where he had landed, "Hello?"

There was no answer.

Unconsciously, he crawled back to the porch and up the three steps. The door was still open and the candle was still lit. He pushed the door and it opened fully.

In the middle of the room, an invitation, a wooden table lit by three candles. Two chairs faced each other. The one nearest him, pulled back as if someone had just left the room or, he hoped, someone had pulled it out for him.

A creak and he glanced to the left. A door closed. Looked like the door to the tower.

"Hello?" he whispered.

No answer.

He wanted to cry.

"Please, help me," he mouthed.

Empty silence answered, wrenching away his memories. Wrenched his memories from him. A flood in reverse; all the swelling joys, all the anticipating moments of great discovery he had known since he could remember. His childhood an unfolding gift of mysterious sights and sounds and feelings open and fresh and alive with newness. The magic of a bird's nest. The wonder of a turtle's shell lying like the rarest treasure of power on a dry creek bed. Even the bellowing of a drunk old man and his own small face buried in a starch-stiff pillowcase. The ache of being right at the cusp of knowing everything, of sharing everything, of waving your hand and making it all *alright* and all dreams come true.

That was the magic he lost. Flowing away from him in this silence. And it had gone so long ago. Yet here it was again. It looked at him from an empty chair and he could not look away. Nothing seemed as obscene as the emptiness of that chair. Or as promising.

The candlelight flared with a gust of wind through the main door, which he turned to and closed. He was here, in the room, completely. No running away. He turned the lock, then walked to the pulled out chair and sat.

Beneath a candlestick was a sheaf of unruled, sepia papers bound in a black ribbon.

With one hand limp in his lap, he pulled on the knot of the ribbon as if it were the last act of a condemned man. The ribbon unfolded as if pulled by invisible hands. With a delicate push he slid the blank cover sheet away and leaned over the table to stare at the first page of the manuscript. Beautiful, handwritten script. But what language was it? He squinted. Leaned forward a little more. Squinted until his eyes were watery slits. Then he saw, and he was reading her words. No, he was hearing her words. A woman's voice clearly speaking to him. Soothing, cradling words. He closed his eyes and the story unfolded. He felt like a boy, a boy alone and waiting for that call in the dark, "Ollie, ollie, oxen free." Come home. Come home.

The Boy Who Found Something of Value

Once upon a time there was a little boy and a little girl who went into the woods looking for food because they were very hungry. Their mother and father had gone into the woods before them, but they never came back. Though the boy and girl were afraid of the woods, they were alone in the world and starving and they had no other choice. For a day and a night they walked through the woods without finding any food. The little girl began to cry, but she didn't show her brother. Hungry and cold they soon fell asleep in a nook under a large oak tree.

When the little boy woke up the next morning his sister was gone. He searched through the woods for her all day and a night. But he could not find her. Finally, cold, hungry, and alone, he threw himself to the ground and fell asleep.

As the sun came up, a giant prowled through the woods looking for something to eat. He found the boy still sleeping. The giant had never seen a boy before. He picked him up and cradled him in the palm of his hand.

"You look like a human, but you're smaller," the giant grumbled. "I wonder if there's any flavor to you?" The giant licked his lips and put the boy into his mouth. But just then a bird flew down from the top of a tree and landed on the giant's shoulder. The bird sang to the giant, "Don't eat the boy. One day he will find something of value."

The giant nodded and said he could use a helper. He decided to take the boy to his castle on the top of a black mountain. The little boy tried his best to be helpful, but he couldn't do giant things. Everything was too big for him. He could never do anything right.

Angry, the giant said it was time for the boy to find something valuable or he would eat the boy up. The giant gave the boy two black strings tied together in a knot. They were giant strings so they formed a big black bag. The giant told the boy to find something useful, put it in the bag, and bring it back to the castle.

But the giant didn't trust the boy, so he sent an ugly imp to accompany him. The imp was told to make sure that anything useful the boy found was brought back to the giant.

That morning the boy set out on the road following the bird who flew overhead to guide him. The imp followed behind the boy throwing rocks at him and calling him names. Whenever anyone heard the boy cry out, the imp made himself invisible and hid behind the boy's ear. He told the boy to say it was just the wind whistling through his ears.

They walked for a day and a night and soon they came across a man who was sitting on the side of the road polishing large nuggets of gold. The boy stopped and watched the man because he looked like the boy's grandfather. The imp threw a rock and hit the boy on the head.

"Ow," he cried out. "Stop that."

The old man stopped polishing the gold and asked what was wrong.

"Nothing, sir," the boy sighed. "It is just the wind whistling through my ears."

"Well, what are you doing out here by yourself?" asked the man, squinting at the boy through thick gold-rimmed glasses.

"My guardian sent me out to find something valuable," the boy said.

"Oh," the man nodded. "Maybe this will help."

He reached inside his vest pocket and pulled out something shiny.

"This should do," the man smiled. He handed the boy a pen fashioned of pure gold. "Whatever story is written with this pen," he continued, "will make people happy and wise and will make the writer very rich."

"Oh, no," the boy shook his head. "I couldn't accept that."

"Why not?" asked the man quite amazed.

"I don't know how to make people happy, wise, or rich, and my guardian told me I had to find something useful," the boy replied.

"Your guardian will know what to do," the man laughed. "I'll write something on this piece of paper for him." The man wrote a note with the pen and gave it to the boy.

The boy accepted the gold pen and the note with a gentle bow of his head. Carefully, he put them into the big black bag and thanked the man again. Then he and the imp headed back to the castle.

But that night in the mountains while the boy slept, the imp stole the gold pen and hid it away. The next day when they got back to the giant's castle the imp told the giant that the boy had lost the gold pen in the forest. The giant asked the boy if it was true. The boy said it wasn't, but when he opened the bag to show the giant the gold pen, it was gone.

"What's this?" asked the giant pointing at the note.

"How to use the gold pen," the boy whispered.

"What good are you?" roared the giant. "How can I use what I don't have, you stupid boy?" He tore up the note and picked up the boy by the scruff of his neck. He started to put the boy in his mouth when the little bird flew down and sat on the giant's shoulder. The bird sang, "Don't eat the boy. One day he will find something of value."

So the boy was sent out on the road again with the bird flying overhead to guide him and the imp following him shouting curses and throwing stones.

They walked for a day and a night and soon they came across an old woman who was spinning silken robes in front of a beautiful cottage. The boy stopped and watched her because she reminded him of his grandmother.

"What are you doing out on the road by yourself?" she asked as she pulled him gently toward her.

The boy told her he was looking for something valuable to bring to his guardian. The woman looked down into her basket of scraps and pulled out a small, red piece of cloth.

"This is a magic cloth," she said. "When you put it on a table the food will taste like it was made by angels and a single bite will make you feel happy and full."

"Ask her for instructions," the invisible imp barked from behind the boy's ear.

"Why do I need instructions?" complained the boy.

"What?" asked the woman.

"Oh, it's just the wind, ma'am, whistling through my ears," the boy said, kicking at the dirt.

The boy asked for instructions and the woman said, "Because you're such a kind boy to help your guardian, I'll also tell you how to spin the magic thread." She wrote the instructions on a piece of paper. The boy thanked the old woman and put the cloth and the note in the big black bag and once again headed back to the giant's castle.

That night while the boy slept the imp stole the cloth. The next day when they got back to the giant's castle the imp told the giant that the boy had lost the magic cloth in the mountains. The giant asked the boy if it was true. Again, the boy said it wasn't, but when he opened the bag to show the giant the magic cloth, it was gone.

"What's this?" sneered the giant pointing at the note.

"How to use the magic cloth," whispered the boy.

"What good are you?" roared the giant. "How can I use what I don't have, you stupid boy?" He tore up the note and picked up the boy by the scruff of his neck. He put the boy in his mouth and was about to bite down when the little bird flew down again and sat on the giant's shoulder. The bird sang, "Don't eat the boy. One day he will find something of value."

So the boy was sent out on the road once more with the bird overhead as guide and the imp skulking behind throwing stones and telling him what a stupid boy he is.

They walked for a day and a night and they came to a crossroads on the top of a mountain. Across the valley they saw a castle that was even bigger than the giant's castle. When they came to the castle there was a terrible smell and bones were scattered all about.

The imp scowled, "Let's leave. This place smells like death."

But the boy didn't move. The imp threw a rock at him, but the boy ducked and the rock missed.

The boy whispered, "I hear someone crying."

He followed the sounds of crying to a small room attached to the side of the castle. A stream filled with giant fish flowed quietly beside the room and into a cave in the side of the mountain. The boy opened the door and was almost blinded. Alone inside, a little girl sat covering her face and crying on a black iron chair. All around her the dirt floor sparkled with thousands of diamonds.

"What's wrong, girl?" asked the little boy softly.

The little girl turned away as if ashamed. "The dragon keeps me here," she sighed. "It comes in here once a week and gathers up my tears and then leaves."

"You can run away with me," the little boy said in an encouraging voice.

"No," she said sadly. "If there is no one in this chair the fish in the stream tell the dragon who lives in the cave and it comes and eats everyone up. Those are the bones you see outside."

"Just get the diamonds," the imp growled from behind the boy's ear.

"No!" shouted the little boy.

"Who are you talking to?" asked the little girl.

The boy shook his head in disgust. "It's just the wind whistling through my ears," he answered.

"Get the diamonds, you stupid boy!" yelled the imp.

"No! No! No!" yelled back the little boy.

"Yes! Yes! Yes!" shouted the imp and he suddenly appeared beside the boy. Startled by the imp's appearance, the girl jumped out of her chair and screamed.

"Sister!" the boy cried out with joy.

"Brother!" his sister answered as she threw her arms around him.

But no sooner had she hugged him when a loud roar shook the room.

"The dragon!" she gasped.

"You can feed the dragon," the imp squealed as he began pushing the girl toward the door. But the boy thought quickly. He picked up a diamond and threw it at the imp. The diamond found its mark and knocked the imp through the doorway. The girl quickly ran to the door and closed it.

The dragon ate the imp and spit out his bones, just like that. It roared again, still ready to eat, but the boy jumped on the chair and the dragon flew back to its cave.

"What are we going to do now?" the little boy asked.

The little girl's eyes lit up. "I have an idea," she said. "Just stay in the chair. I'll be right back."

She walked outside and gathered up the bones of the imp. She stuffed them all into the giant's black bag. She went back to the room and said to the boy, "When I tell you to, jump out of the chair."

"I'm ready," grinned the boy.

"Now!" the girl shouted.

The boy jumped from the chair. Then his sister quickly, but very carefully, placed the bag of bones right in the middle of the chair where the boy had sat. The dragon opened one fiery eye, then smiled a dragonish grin and curled back to enjoy its delectable dreams.

The reunited brother and sister hugged and kissed each other, their eyes filling with tears of joy. Then they stuffed their pockets full of diamonds and went over the far side of the mountains where they found a new home and lived happily ever after.

* * *

The man woke. He was crying. Sitting in the room crying. The candles were still burning. No smaller than when he'd stepped into the tower in what seemed to be hours before.

He was weak. Hands helped him to his feet.

"Shh. You'll be fine. Come back tomorrow night. I'll tell you more."

He slowly turned to face the voice. It was her. He knew it was her.

He was floating.

"Tomorrow. You'll know how to find me tomorrow."

"How did you…?" he whispered. He had just been thinking how to find her again. He had no idea where he was or how he got there.

"You'll know," he heard again and he was standing on a grassy ridge looking at the cottage. The night was full of stars raining down from the sky, streaking its velvet blue with gold fire. And the stars fell and fell, there was no stopping them falling. An infinity of golden stars raining from the sky. And there, far below him beside a silver blue sea, the tower rose with a single window visible. Her shadow passed behind the window and the stars stopped falling and night collapsed around him.

He heard a coyote howl. He turned and he was standing next to his Jeep. His hand throbbing, swollen.

He turned again and there was only the sea shining in the mundane starry darkness beyond the rolling hills and the deeper, lightless darkness of the forest, a darkness that filled him with dread.

He got in his Jeep and drove north. An hour later he pulled into a community hospital parking lot and checked himself in. Two fingers broken. He asked for sedatives. They prescribed extra strength Tylenol. He felt the power of those punishing waves rising from the dark island of his heart. Smiling sweetly, he asked for something with a tad more kick. His was a small dragon of a pain, he knew, but a dragon which nonetheless required more than a safety pin for a sword. That's what he wanted to say. It may even have been what he said, for he wanted a rest, a real long sleeping vacation.

But something about his old mannerisms had lost its charm.

Time to begin a new campaign.

He started screaming. The administrators agreed to put him under observation for three days.

But three days was it. He didn't sleep well at all. And then the insurance companies kicked in. He could go to jail if he chose, but his insurance company would have no more of his laying about asking nurses for shots of diamonds and bones and NASA maps of coastal California.

On the fourth day he was back in his Jeep and looking for a cottage with a black tower attached somewhere off 101.

The Dragon Beneath the Castle

He didn't find the tower that night when he left the hospital. Nor the next day nor the next. Up and down the coastal highway he traveled looking for a way over that mountain range and into the world that boy had found. He wanted a way out, a way in.

Nothing. Nothing except the muscles along the top of his spine ached with a pain he hadn't known since he couldn't remember.

It felt like a sword was sheathed just to the left of his right shoulder blade. Rested like it lived there, like it had always lived there and it was only now, now that he was so desperately in need of peace that he noticed it.

Ironic, he thought.

And then, "I hate irony."

He imagined if he twisted or rolled his shoulders ever so, just so, just—you know—a bit more to the...just there. If he could just feel a little more self-loathing so that it would pierce his heart.

Dead. Then he could relax. No. Not that. Not yet. It wasn't his time.

It was time for something else.

An Arthur was who he needed. Some boy to pluck the damned thing from his back. To slip the thing from his imprisoning flesh and let it sing fully in the light of the larger world, surely a more appreciative audience.

He winced. The tension was killing him.

Being a stone was tiresome. Being a sword in the stone was intolerable.

Unfortunately, he heard no voices telling him that he was Arthur as well as sword and stone.

He had figured out that triad himself, but such a holistic trump didn't really work quite as sweetly as he thought such cleverness might.

Cleverness. A cheap trick. An old trick. It might have worked for Hermes, who talked his way into the graces of Zeus with his clever lies, but he was no Hermes and these times were of a different mythic timbre. Cleverness was cowardice as far as he figured it. Plot twists for the easily amused, for the heroes who hedged their bets with life insurance and a pay or play contract.

Life was murkier than that. There were few if any elegant segues into and out of the kind of crappy situations he had witnessed in his few years on this cowtown planet.

Cynicism was poisoning him, but he couldn't stop himself. Maybe it was what he needed, he would tell himself in an uncharacteristic fit of optimism.

Poison was the ticket. Get so low that the basest of survival mechanisms would kick in.

No, he wanted the voices. Wanted some hint of a way out that wasn't ironic or desperate or tinged with an organic stench of philosophical materialism.

But on the really bad days he would settle for better analgesics.

Ten days passed before the pain became excruciating enough for him to get into his Jeep and head for the hospital again. Extra strength caplets and hourly affirmations just weren't doing the trick. Cleverness had been outstripped by misery.

It was raining. It was dark. And he took a left when he should have taken a right and he was there. The tower shone like a snake skin staff of the gods, defiant in the lightning flashes that webbed the brooding blue of heaven over the churning Pacific waters.

There wasn't much fight in him. The pain crawled up and down his spine like a hungry piranha. He could see the door was open. The candles were lit.

And she was sitting with her back to him. Sitting and holding something up just high enough over her right shoulder for him to see that it was a card or a small book. Tarot cards, he guessed. A reading for him. He felt it as surely as he felt the damned sword twist toward his heart.

He had to step out of the Jeep and walk to the tower. He had to. His head dropped to the top of the steering wheel. He was crying. But it wasn't the pain in his back. He raised his head and said, "I have to. I have to. The sword…will be pulled…if I…just…open the door."

He didn't move. He sat there and rocked gently back and forth, glancing down at the lights of his dashboard then up at the distant candlelight.

Up and down and back and forth. And his feet tapping on the accelerator and the brake. Tap right, tap left. Back and forth. Down and up. Tap, tap, back and down, forth and up, tap tap, back and down, back and down….

And the tears dried on his cheeks as his lids grew heavy and the lights glistened through the salty liquid of his eyes and he heard a voice whispering as if on his radio. The green blue lights of his radio pulsed gently and a woman's voice tap, tap, and then a sweet, relaxing flow like water on a stone…a voice like water finding a gap between the sword and the stone….

***

Once upon a time there was a prince who was called upon in his youth to go to a magic castle in a faraway land. It was foretold by an ancient wizard of the silent wood that the inhabitants of this castle would welcome the prince when he gave to them a golden ring and a silver key.

But the wizard had warned that there was more than merely the giving required for the prince's quest to be successful. The ring and key had to be presented to the people of the castle at a time and in a fashion that would bind the moment in their long and brimming memories as an event worth remembering forever.

The young prince, brash and full of pride, thought nothing of such a feat. A quest of this nature would be easy enough to accomplish he boasted to all the court. After all, he had a flair for acting and dance and the way he plucked the strings of the lyre bettered anyone in the kingdom. With such an arsenal, how could he fail, he wanted to know? The wizard bowed to the prince's bravado and said, with a wan smile, that the prince surely would become the object of much talk in this faraway land renowned for its exquisite beauty and wisdom deeper than the wells of time.

The prince smiled at his agreement and turned to accept gifts from his royal parents. His father presented to him a golden ring that had been won by his father in combat with infidels many years earlier. The prince put the ring in a black velvet pouch and turned to face his mother. His mother then gifted him a silver key, kissing it before it fell from her small white hands into the black pouch She had been given the key by a priestess of the moon when the queen first bloomed to womanhood. The prince pulled the gold string tight and hung the pouch beneath his shirt next to his heart. He refused all other gifts or offers from the court's youthful company. They clamored to adventure with him, but he set out alone on his beautiful chestnut stallion to find this castle said by the wizard to stand on a high promontory fast by a blue-green sea. The whole kingdom gathered to see him off at dawn on the first day of spring. Many a knight followed him to the edge of the last sheep-grazed meadow before the prince waved them off with a flash of his beribboned arm. On his own, he entered the unnamed land beyond.

The prince traveled many months through forbidding forests and parched deserts. He slipped in and out of wolf-ridden valleys and over bitterly cold mountains. Twice he crossed wave-tossed and storm-bitten seas before he finally found a ship full of pirates knowledgeable of hidden things and willing to take him into the waters of the forbidden silver sea on whose shores waited the faraway castle of his destiny.

Over the long months of travels he had lost nearly everything he had brought with him. His beautiful show horse died in a hard ride across a burning steppe. The prince's once elegant clothing had become threadbare through his careless adventuring and his inattention to simple tasks his servants had always performed for him. A scraggly wanderer's beard covered his handsome face. His light blond hair had grown long and dark with soot and oil from too many campfires. His eyes were dark and baggy from short, uncomfortable sleeps in foul-smelling inns and rat-infested ships.

Still, he had the gold ring and silver key. These he faithfully pulled from his black pouch each morning and evening. They were the first and last things he saw everyday.

At dawn with the low tide, a young pirate, barely twelve, rowed the prince to the closest shore. The boy grunted his thanks for the gold coins the prince tossed into the bottom of the boat. It was the last of his money. He jumped into the surf as mottled seals bellied to the water for their first meal. The boy just shook his head in mocking pity as he pulled the small rowboat away from the shore.

The prince pushed his way through the waves to the beach and smiled as he looked up the steep face of a black cliff. Hesitating only long enough to take a long, deep breath he immediately set to climbing. An hour later he stood on the black promontory gazing westward at the castle he had come so far to claim. It was magnificently mysterious, shrouded in a swirling mist upon a white cliff on the far side of a great, blue-green bay.

The prince laughed out loud.

All in all, he was surprised and quite pleased with himself to have found the castle in such a relatively short time. It had only cost him a year or so, a horse, some clothes, a few coins, and a little vanity. It was nothing he could not easily replace once he became king of faraway. He stretched his arms wide into the strong and steady wind and smiled triumphantly. Then he pulled out the pouch with the ring and key and gestured challengingly toward the castle. Soon, he thought. Very soon this will all be mine. He placed the pouch back against his chest and headed into the dark forest in the direction of the castle.

The journey lasted longer than he imagined it would take when he had first stood gazing from the wind-swept promontory, so it happened that the prince came to his destination very late into the night. Though the bridge over the moat was down, the great carved gate to the castle was closed. As far as he could see no lights were visible. Everyone in the castle and its environs seemed to be asleep.

The prince shrugged off the silence and the dark. He pulled his hair back and proudly walked up to the gate, raised his hand to knock, but then he hesitated. Perhaps, this was bad timing, he thought. Indeed, he was unknown here. He did not want to appear rude. His first encounter with these people who he would soon rule should be one that would not leave them with the wrong impression. After all, he was not an irresponsible lout who pounded upon a castle's gate at any hour that suited him. No, such a man could not rule the kind of kingdom the prince imagined for himself. He turned away from the gate.

The prince decided he would make a bed of branches on the other side of the moat and greet his would-be subjects at break of day. Day one, he wistfully thought, of the reign of a king whose name would become unmatched in tales of heroism and glory. He gathered some pine boughs from the nearby stand and then lay on his back and studied the moon until he fell asleep and began dreaming.

He dreamed of his future as that great and powerful king sitting in a gold throne shaped like a small caravel. He sneered as he watched kings and queens of lesser lands bow before him and speak his name in tones of awe and trembling wonder. He was proud and tall and handsome—unconquerable. But from somewhere near the middle of the courtyard he heard a rumbling and a swirl of dry dust rising from the marbled floor. Suddenly in the midst of the magnificent castle there loomed a huge and terrible dragon rising up before him in a green horror. The winged snake opened its blood-dripping maw and sent out a red black spume of roiling fire that tore open the ground at the king's feet. Snakes of red-hot lava curled, striking with a fierce and burning breath around the feet of the courtiers and their ladies. The earth shuddered once and swallowed the king in a hissing of white steam and pitiless roaring.

The prince awoke with a start. His first thought was of the ring. The ring and the key. He reached for his pouch. It was gone. He sat up. He was freezing. He was naked in the snow. Moon-lit footprints led away from where he sat and far into the woods. He ran a few steps then stopped, deeply ashamed. He could see the rosy breath of dawn edging over the white-skinned sea. He took a few steps back toward the castle and raised his shivering hand to knock, but was again frozen in shame. Soon the gate would open and they would find him naked and alone with nothing to prove he was their future king. He looked up and saw a young woman's eyes looking at him. His face flushed deep red. He turned and ran into the woods and ran and ran until he could run no further and he collapsed unconscious beneath a black weaving of barren oak branches.

All he remembered later was snatches of fiery eyes and white dust smoke rising from a black labyrinth of volcanic chasms. He was hot, burning, and running, ever running from those eyes. It felt like years of falling, thinking he was awake and then being trapped in a chasm with those eyes rising in the white dust smoke. Endlessly these images hounded him in a dream he felt would never change.

Then, inexplicably, he was awake, eyes wide, crusty and blood-shot; dry-mouthed and shivering with a fever, wrapped in a goat's skin and surrounded by several strange looking people. Their faces were dark and covered with worn scarves, bright red and green, leaving only their eyes and foreheads visible. Everything smelled of oak fires. They smiled weakly at him and an old woman put to his mouth a spoonful of warm goat's milk mixed with something sweet and bitter. He grimaced but swallowed and fell back into a wonderfully dreamless sleep.

Over the next few days and weeks he learned through the gesturings and crude drawings of his old woman caretaker that he had been discovered near death deep in the forest. His rescuers were a wandering band of cask and casket makers. They were foreigners from over the sea who spoke a foreign tongue, but they were kind to him and never insisted he work even weeks after he was up and about.

The prince could not bring himself to speak. He learned their language quickly and sometimes wanted to thank them, especially the old woman, but the words just would not come. They were happy people who sang and danced every night. They always asked him to join them around the fire, but he always declined, preferring to stand in the shadow of the trees listening to their Gypsy songs and crying silently.

Months passed and he eventually joined the circle. One night he gestured to the mandolin of the chief player asking if he could be allowed to play. The chief player shrugged and handed the instrument to the silent guest with an air of bemused resignation. The prince studied the instrument, plucked a few strings awkwardly which brought laughs all around. The prince nodded modestly at the playful derision, then adjusted the tuning and began to play.

When he finished playing they all jumped to their feet with tears in their eyes and hugged him with great joy. He had become a true Gypsy, they declared, and would always be welcome wherever true hearts reigned. The prince smiled weakly at their admiration, but excused himself to sleep under the old woman's wagon. The friendly nomads shook their heads in pity for the young melancholy prince but not one ever said a thing. All ways are God's ways they said to each other and they turned back to the fire. The old woman began singing a love's lament.

Many more months passed as the prince wandered with the Gypsies through strange lands. He finally found the courage to speak, but only to the old woman who taught him the tricks of cask making and of the medicinal uses of plants. He was a quick learner and he was generous with his caring. Many a father thought he would make a good son-in-law and many a maiden would sit beside him at the fire. Still he felt like an outsider and refused all offers of help or pay from any, save the old woman.

One crisp fall day the Gypsies stopped at a small, well maintained farm house. The fields on either side of the road as far as the prince could see were covered in grape vines. The owner of the vineyard, an old aristocratic wine maker came out to inspect the oaken casks offered in barter. After a bit of haggling the trade was made and a milk goat, a few geese, and some bottles of wine exchanged. The prince could see the wine maker gesturing back and forth between the prince and the fields. The Gypsies called the old woman over and in a few moments there were nods of agreement all around. The old woman shook the wine maker's hand three times. Another goat and more bottles were passed off.

The old woman slowly walked over to the prince and gently held his face in her hands. Silently she looked long into his eyes and then kissed him on both cheeks, looked again and walked back to the wine maker. She pressed something into his palm. She turned back to the prince and gestured for him to close his eyes. When he opened them again the prince was standing alone with the wine maker. The Gypsies' wagons were far down the road.

The prince wasn't saddened by the fact that the old woman had traded him to the wine maker. He owed her and the Gypsies his life. Disappointment was his lot in life he thought. It wasn't an unfair bargain as far as he could see. With a slight shrug of the shoulders he agreed to stay with the wine maker for as long as necessary. The wine maker nodded his hardy approval and set the prince to work in the fields.

Years passed and the prince worked uncomplainingly in the fields. His work and the errands the wine maker assigned him brought the prince into contact with the local village people and slowly he was accepted into their community. Once it became known that the prince was a healer and could play the lyre better than anyone they had ever heard, the villagers were always asking him to tend to their sick and play for their festivals and other events.

The wine maker encouraged the prince in these activities. It was the wine maker who introduced the prince to a beautiful young woman, daughter of the miller. Though the prince fell in love with the young woman, he would not ask to marry her and she dare not ask him. They would meet and talk once a week at the village well and that seemed to be enough for both of them as the years passed.

The prince had proved himself worthy in his field work and in his relations with the villagers so the old wine maker decided to teach him the secrets of wine making. The prince was an astute pupil, still, it took him many years to learn how to make truly good wine. When the master finally said he was ready, he knew he truly was.

He had become a master himself, and his wine, the old wine maker said, was good enough to be served to the king himself, something the old wine maker had never accomplished. He said that since such a wine had not been made in many years it must be reserved for the king. The wine maker said he himself was too old and unworthy to make such a delivery to the king. The prince would have to the deliver the wine himself.

Thus early one cold and windy morning the prince readied the wagon with four casks of royal wine. The old wine maker gave him a crudely drawn map with the directions to the king's castle and patted the prince on the back with tender, fatherly concern. He never said a word and turned his cheek away when the prince offered a kiss goodbye. The old man slipped something into the prince's pocket as the prince climbed into the creaky wagon. The prince nodded farewell and the horse pulled away.

When he got to the bend in the road, he turned to look at the farm, but a fog had rolled in behind him and it was as if the farm had never been there. The prince sighed and drove on into the forest.

It was after dark when he finally approached the castle. A cold fear swept over him as if he had fallen into an icy well. It was the castle. The castle he had set out to find all those years ago. He pulled the wagon to a sudden stop and stared at the once beautiful vision he had abandoned in shame and terror those many years ago. What was he to do now?

Knock? Wait until the morning? Run away again? Be found naked by a band of thieving Gypsies?

He breathed deeply to calm himself. What would it matter now if he knocked after night? He was just a wine maker. A simple wine maker. He laughed softly and got down from the wagon. His horse whinnied and he reached in his pocket for a sugar cube he always kept to reward the horse for a good day's pull. What is this, he thought as he pulled out a small package, a note tied with string. He unwrapped the note and the key and the ring from his youth fell to the ground. He just stared at them for a second unbelieving, confused. He looked at the note. It read: When you need us, call.

The prince leaned against a cask of wine, dizzy, his ears ringing, his jaw clenched so hard to keep from weeping that his cheeks vibrated. He had been plunged into a deep well of sorrow, but as he struggled against its pull the black tears edged closer to the surface and the sorrow turned to a rage he could barely dam at his throat. All those years. All those years. He turned and glared at the shadowed gate. His hands knotted into tight oak burls of anger. He wanted to tear the castle down stone by stone. A cask of wine. A cask of wine, his gift to the king. A life for a cask of wine.

The securing rope was ripped from the wagon hook as if it were merely a spider's thread. With one quick, inhuman motion he threw the cask against the gate in a volcanic fury. All the years he had spent on this fool's quest. And as he let the cask fly he screamed his own name, the most damnable curse he knew.

The cask struck the door full on but it did not shatter. It did not explode in the red river of regrets the prince had expected. The door was not locked. It swung open and from its shadowy mouth terrifying, piercing screams poured forth in a howling black wind that knocked the startled prince to his knees. The sounds were so inhuman, so horrifically painful, he pulled at his ears as if to tear them off, to stop any sound from penetrating. The screaming wind swirled around him like a living tornado. He could see, or rather feel, hundreds of faces, contorted and skeletal, eyes wide with mouths stretched open enough to swallow him whole. They wrapped themselves around his body, entering him, trying to puncture him, rip him apart from inside. They were relentless, cruel, and he felt himself falling into their cold, judging arms. He wanted to die but they would not take him. They only wanted to torment him with his own unforgiving shame. And so he cried and cried.

It was several minutes, an eternity of crying, before he found that he wanted to open his eyes, to see, if for the last time, the place where his dreams began and ended. The screaming tornado still tore all around him, but he was calmer now, ready to face whatever it was. He opened his eyes. The screams stopped all at once as if cut with a sword and everything was utterly silent.

At first all he saw were motes of light swirling, jumping with his every blink. When he squeezed his eyes tight to clear them he could see the screaming faces again but they were much further away. Still, they were racing straight at him as if they were hurtling down a long, thin, black tunnel with a flowering claw of red and yellow fire at their heels. He opened his eyes wide. The faces evaporated. Moonlight spread itself across the castle wall like a thin veil of fairy milk and his vision cleared. He saw the wine cask unbroken, still rocking in an empty, dusty hall. The door moved slightly on its ancient hinges. Not so much as a dent reflected on its smooth surface.

The prince stood and walked to the threshold. He leaned in, grabbed the handle and solemnly pulled the door shut.

Standing there, his nose inches from the door, he stared at the grain of the wood. It was good wood he thought. Oak. A strong oak door. It would have made a fine cask.

He took a deep breath and raised his right arm with his hand in a tight fist. He breathed a little deeper. His fist relaxed and he knocked three times. One. Two. Three. He waited for three breaths then raised his hand to knock again. Deep breath. Footsteps. Breath caught in his throat. His jaw clenched. He leaned a little closer and turned his ear to the door. Slow. Faint. Echoes of footsteps.

The door opened and the prince stepped back, his skin burning with a rash of nameless fear.

A bent old woman stepped into the moon-sprayed square of light carved by the open door and stopped and swayed as if moved by the subtle currents of the strange night's air. She was terribly thin, dressed in a long black gown with a black lace shawl covering her head and draped around her shoulders. It trailed in a thick, chalky dust that covered the stone floors. She slowly lifted the veil and tears glistened in every crease of her sunken cheeks. The prince squinted. There was something he remembered in those eyes.

"You," she said, her voice thin, worn with an age he could not imagine, a voice he thought that seemed little more than a dying whisper. He reached out to hold her frail arm, which slowly raised to point to his chest. But she turned away, shaking her head in nervous, small movements, as if she were wracked with pain. He took a step and she turned to face him, this time with an anger in her eyes.

"What took you so long?" she asked, her voice quavering but with a regal air that shamed him. "Why didn't you come? We waited and waited for you. I was there at the window waiting for you to come in. All you had to do was push. It was open all the time. All these years. All you had to do was push. All you ever had to do was walk up to the door and push. All you had to do was call out. See what you have done with your pride?"

The prince fell to his knees and wept beyond the weeping he had earlier thought was unbearable. This time he wept so that his body shook uncontrollably. He fell forward to rest on his hands. He was a shaggy beast swaying in abject fear and a grief that would empty the seas. His flesh could not bear the trembling and he collapsed—a frightened, weeping seed-child in the dust of the ancient hall. No demon faces pressed to devour him. No fire-laced tornadoes tore at his shame-filled soul. There was only an endless blackness, a void beyond reckoning.

The door shut behind him with the thundering force of a stone coffin dropped from heaven onto the cold surface of hell's own funeral. The prince raised his face to where the old woman had stood but she was gone. Not even her footprints were visible, no trace of her shawl dragged through the grey dust. He was utterly alone in the emptiness of the doomed castle. He stood like a new-born colt, wet, wobbly, disoriented. He stumbled down the hall toward the center of his abandoned dream.

A beam of moonlight from a high window fell upon a torch anchored on a gold-painted wall. In a brass lion's paw beneath the anchor lay two flame-shaped striking stones. The prince lit the torch and held it against the blackness of the ancient halls.

Cobwebs were everywhere, covering every edge of the high ceiling halls and rooms. Spiders, red, black, yellow, white, blue, pulsated in anticipation as he passed down corridor after corridor of decay. Skeletons in gowns, waistcoats and brocade breeches, glass slippers, leather boots, stockings, feathers, skins and bells, silver armor, course sackcloth, ladies, servants, courtiers, children, knights, peasants sat in velvet chairs, sofas or lay on the marble floors as if they simply had curled in sleep and never woke. Room after room offered the same sights. Beauty and grace beyond compare covered in dust and cobwebs, rotting, wasted.

He came to stairs leading to the tower of the keep. He looked up the spiral staircase. A faint, watery light quavered against a muraled wall. This time there was no fear in him. This time his heart raced with hope, with a desire to find life, any life, his life.

A door at the top of the stairs was open slightly. He scanned the floor for footprints. There were none. Where was she? He pushed the door further and raised the torch high.

Inside the room was a gold carriage, eight gold horses harnessed, manes tossed in an imaginary wind, a gold coachman, four footmen hanging on golden rails. Inside the coach sat a white-faced king and queen facing forward and two equally death-white young princesses facing their parents. They were not gold, but living images dressed all in white and covered in a white dust, alive, living ghosts, their thin chests rising ever so slightly with their heads bowed and eyes closed. It appeared they were sleeping sitting up.

The prince edged forward and whispered a hello. The princess nearest him turned her head slightly and lifted her blood red-rimmed eyelids, dust falling, and floating in the stirred air as she moved. She blinked once slowly and again, then turned her head back down.

"I'm not a dream," the prince said more loudly. He took a step forward. "I'm not a dream. I'm sorry. I've come to make it right. I've come to lift the curse, to clear your dull, dust-filmed eyes so they can meet mine, to make amends. I've learned. Listen."

The prince ran to the door and threw back his head and screamed as loud as he could, "Come to me. I need you. I am calling for help. I need help. You said you would come. Come now!"

He looked down the stairs, listening, holding his breath. The mysterious light that danced on the walls vanished. The castle plunged into pitch darkness. Everything was utterly silent. Not even a mote of dust fell in the golden carriage. He didn't move. He stood there, rigid.

He could feel the red-rimmed eyes of the princess on him, could imagine the white powdered face, the high white hair, the thin bloodless lips. The slow re-closing of the eyes as if he, too, would fade in the eternal dreaming nightmare of her frozen childhood. Everything dead in life. No one coming with the fire of a new time. The air so cold it voided even his own scent. The air stank like a tomb unopened for a thousand years. And this silence, this deathly scream of silence reigned because of him.

A single tear rolled down his cheek, and his lips almost imperceptibly moved, formed the words please, please come and he closed his eyes, took a deep breath and waited for the dust to settle on him as it had the others, another sentinel for the golden carriage to take him to a wedding that would never be…there…what's that? A whisper of music. A sound as thin as a string of gossamer ribboned in a child's hair. His eyes widened, he breathed in sharply and said a little louder, "Yes." The ribbon became a flag. "Yes," he called louder and took a step into the hall.

Music flooded in a rush into the castle bearing a luscious golden light on its ethereal wings, bursting into the rooms and racing down the halls like a torrent of heavenly fire. Singing and playing flutes and lyres, the Gypsies, the prince's rescuers and slavers, both, danced into view from every corner of the enchanted castle as if they had always been there, had been the very spiders the prince had feared. The prince's own casks of wine were rolled in, but there were hundreds of them instead of a few. The servants tapped them and hundreds of hands reached with generous goblets into the spouting fountains of wine. Overflowing goblets spilled onto the lips of the skeletons. The magic of the wine flooded across their bones. They stood brittle bones and danced themselves back into flesh, their cheeks suddenly roses, their eyes bright, piercing fires.

The prince spun around and around in a kaleidoscope of dazzling vision and wonder. He laughed with tears pouring from his eyes as plentiful as the wine pouring into every mouth, down chin and breast and to the floor, which shone with the light of the sea on fire. Someone told him the castle well had been uncovered and that the deep, pure waters had channeled themselves into the castle to wash away all the years of waiting dust. Everyone came up to him with eyes shining and smiles of great joy, kissing him and hugging him and toasting his good health. He was delighted beyond measure. Time had stopped again but in paradise and he was where he belonged.

"Yes," he said and raised his head to the stained-glass skylight high above him. A pulsing white beam of starlight pierced the center of the window and it shot past his head like a bolt of lightning. He turned as if to catch it.

The white-gowned princess of the golden carriage stood before him. The prince's lips parted but closed quickly and he knelt before her on one knee, his head bowed. She waited for three breaths then gently touched his chin to raise his face to hers. Neither of them spoke. She stared into his eyes for the longest time. Without breaking her gaze she called out to a footman. She turned her head slightly and whispered to the servant. The servant walked to a case behind the prince and pulled from its interior a magnificent jewel-handled sword.

The prince never broke eye contact with her. She was more beautiful than he could say and his heart melted and belonged to her as if it were her own heart. He reached out to her hand and brought it to his lips, kissed it passionately and pressed it to his wet cheek.

"No," she said. "It is not over." She pointed to a closed door behind the carriage. "You must go down and deal with the dragon."

"Yes," he said, rising immediately. "Yes, I know."

The prince took the sword from the servant and walked to the carriage. He bowed to the three royals still inside. They nodded their approval, then turned their eyes to the closed door. The prince said nothing. He took two steps and pushed it open. Another servant handed him a lit torch.

Quietly the prince stepped into the dark, narrow passage and closed the door behind him.

The passage had stairs carved into it leading down, ever down in a tight spiral, narrowing as he descended. The walls were honeycombed with niches filled with coppery asps and white centipedes that fled before his torch. The passage narrowed until the stairs disappeared and finally the prince had to crawl upon his belly on a slick, muddy floor. He shivered as he crawled.

This was the tunnel where the screaming faces lived. Breathe, he told himself. Breathe and don't close your eyes, no matter how black it may get. He thought then only of the princess, of how his heart knew what it had never known.

Hours passed, but at last the tunnel ended. It ended with a dazzling explosion of light. The tunnel emptied into a huge cavern, its floor covered in a lake several feet below the tunnel's entrance. The black waters reflected the light from the prince's torch unto the sides of the cavern which were encrusted with thousands upon thousands of jewels of every hue and color.

The prince grimaced, covered his eyes with the blade of the sword, but he did not close them. A few quick blinks and they adjusted to the brilliant unearthly light. As he lowered the blade, he could see across from where he crouched a green dragon tied to a golden chain. A ring, also gold, held tightly around its neck.

The old dragon raised its head and sniffed, its eyes closed, crusty. It sniffed again and then slowly its eyes opened, the crust falling to the ground with a sound of breaking glass. The dragon glared at the prince with a yellow eye.

It roared like a mountain breaking open and sent a blue jet of flame arcing high above the pool, but the flame fell short of its mark and spluttered into the hissing waters. The dragon tried to lift itself with its legs but they had grown so thin and weak in their disuse that it could not rise. It stretched its wings but they left their folds no more than a hand's breadth before they fell back to the dragon's dry, scaly sides.

The prince looked for a ledge to walk to the other side and put the poor beast out of its misery, but there was no way. He decided he must swim across the lake. He stripped off his clothing and with sword in hand he dived into the frigid waters.

White fish immediately surrounded him. They suckled at his skin, nipping and gnawing at his flesh. He slapped with his sword and drove them away, but in a moment they were at him again, more viciously, their hunger grown stronger with his resistance. He thrust his sword into the largest of the fish and raised its thick, cold body above his head. He whipped the sword and cut the fish in two. From its stomach fell a silver key which flew through the air and landed beside the dragon's belly. The remaining fish tore into the body of their dead leader and the prince pulled himself unto the shore where the beast lay.

The wyrm raised its head and opened its jaws in a hollow gesture of defiance for no fire issued from its mouth. Its teeth were yellow, moldy, crumbling like watery sand. It turned and stretched its neck out toward the lake, let its great head fall into the roiling waters.

The prince stood and walked to the beast. He picked up the key and put it in his mouth. He raised his sword. The dragon raised its head once, sniffing at the air as if to hold it like a charm, and then closed its eyes and slowly lowered itself again into the water.

The prince hesitated for a heart beat and then his sword fell swiftly and cut the chain from the wall in a shower of sparks. He spit out the key and turned the lock on the golden ring clasped around the dragon's neck. There was a tremendous explosion that knocked the prince to the ground. The rock walls crumbled at once, a vapor of dead skin plaster and salty grit. The water hissed and boiled and the cavern filled with blinding white mist.

A knife-sharp roar cut into the prince's ears, but this time he kept his eyes open. A fluttering of birds crisscrossed about his head, a whirlwind of white doves. Slowly, the ground beneath him rose as if it were breathing, as if it were fingers of earth kneading up into the dark and steamy air like an army of gnawing snakes. Then it cracked open in a thousand places and he was falling, falling….

He closed his eyes and curled as if to sleep forever….

Another loud explosion pounded him. The shock shot through his backbone, into his throat, filled his chest with a surge of golden energy. His chin thrust up, his eyes opened wide. Awake.

The prince found himself upon the golden carriage, a throne with wheels, on top of the mountains of heaven. He looked down into the crowd that fanned out into the valley far below. They were his subjects, the restored inhabitants of the castle and its lands and all the friends he had made in his twenty year wait to push open the castle that was always his to claim.

Even the pirates were there, eating honeycombs and drinking the sweetest of wines that dripped from vines growing like fingers of grass stretching to the sky from below his feet to the furthest horizons.

He looked out onto the verdant fields and deep forests, upon the wide, blue rivers running toward the distant, wave-laced sea. Everything was rich and fertile and gleamed with honey and sweet milk. It had always been his. All he had to do was listen to the call.

He heard another roar and he looked behind him and above to a golden dragon, fierce and wild, its wings outspread to cover half the sky, its head thrown back and roaring to brighten even the sun. Astride the dragon she sat, the white princess, the old Gypsy woman, the miller's daughter at the well, the lady in black, beautiful and powerfully serene. The crowd roared its approval. The prince smiled.

"You," he said.

The Man Who Wanted Everything

The voice called his name.

He jerked his head from the steering wheel. It was still raining, harder than ever and the trees all around groaned in the fury of the storm. His headlights were off and no lights shone on his dash. He felt at the steering column for the key in the ignition. It was there, turned to off.

Absolute darkness surrounded him. Not even the distant lightning, mother to the rumbling he felt more than heard from miles above him, penetrated the void. He strained to see into the distance, but if the tower were really there it was darkened now, hidden in the driving rain with no candle lights to mark its presence.

But the pain had vanished as well. Gone, almost without a trace.

He smiled.

Gone, except for the memory. Except for the story. And her voice.

The smile disappeared.

He opened the door and stepped into the rain. He reached back in the cab and switched on the headlights.

The tower was there.

He reached behind his seat, and without looking, popped the top of his toolbox and grabbed his flashlight. He turned the lights off, shut the door and started walking.

He was scared to death, but he had to know who she was.

The door opened when his foot touched the porch. She stood in the doorway with a candle in her hand.

"It took you awhile, but you're here now. That is what you wanted and this is what you have. You cannot come in now, but you will come tomorrow after dusk and the next day and the next and for as long as you need to come. And I will be here. You will not be lost again. Not when it comes to me. Not when it concerns the tower. You have found me. Now go home. Sleep. You are not crazy and this is not a dream. Good night."

And the door shut.

He stood there for a few seconds trying to remember what she looked like. A veil. She wore a veil and a long black dress. Emily Dickinson, he thought. Emily with a veil. Emily on steroids.

The rain lessened as he stepped back and looked more closely at the tower. It was real enough. He looked again at the door.

"Tomorrow? Okay."

And he came the next day after the light had faded from the sky and she was there and she sat with him in silence for an hour.

And the day after that he asked her a few questions to which she gave nary a straight answer.

The third day she asked him to tell her something he was afraid of.

"Nothing," he grinned.

"So you're afraid of everything?"

She asked the question without the slightest hint of irony or condescension.

"Yes," he responded flatly and more honestly than he expected or even wanted.

"Then we'll begin there. Do you like to swim?" she asked.

"Yes, I do," he answered slowly, deliberately.

"Really?" her voice smiled skeptically, pressing the question and leaning a little closer to him. The veil barely moved with her breath. The question caught him, a soft blow to his brittle ego.

Why would she doubt him on this? He smiled tightly, a defensive anger rising within him. A twinge hit his right shoulder. He reached across his heart and pressed the sore shoulder with his fingertips. He could see himself stroking through the cold water at night, far out to sea, the moonlight electric on the lips of the small breaking waves. The white tips lurking beneath the surface, hungry.

He was terrified. His eyes glanced quickly at the impenetrable veil.

Her eyes held him for a few seconds. He could always see her eyes even when she insisted they meet in the darkness at the foot of the staircase within the tower itself. Her eyes held him and then she looked to the table. She traced the edge of the table top with the tip of a forefinger, back and forth in a slow, gentle stroke, hypnotic, fascinating. His body swayed with every movement, back and forth, back and forth.

The candle light, always dim, suddenly brightened, freezing him in a tense, breathless attention. For a moment he saw ripples of ocean water wave across the table's surface, moonlight quivering on the soft crests, and the shadows of gulls turning, turning.

"Are you tired?" she continued, her hand now stroking the air a few inches above the table as if she were fanning invisible clouds. The table sharpened into solid form again.

He sighed in relief, but his resolve was melting. He held his lungs empty for a second before drawing deeply in through his nostrils. She was taking him there again and he did not want to go.

He spit out the words: "It's not about him." He inhaled another sharp breath, held it, lowered his chin, narrowed his eyes. A hawk. He imagined himself as a hawk, a raptor who could frighten its enemies with its piercing eyes and could rise in swift flight above any danger. He ordered himself to stand and fight, but his breath softened and his body began to sway. "A hawk," he whispered.

His will ran neither hot nor cold. It was lukewarm water misting in a dying night. She controlled him. He would rise only at her bequest. It was what he wanted; what he loathed beyond measure.

"Why did you come then?" she whispered and swayed her head and shoulders, dancing with an invisible lover.

Another sigh escaped him and then a silence wrapped its humid arms across his chest. She knew everything. It wasn't her he loathed. It was his need of her, of her knowledge about him, knowledge always just out of his reach.

His eyes searched the cards on the table but nothing held his gaze. Everything dissolved when he looked too closely. The distinctions of his life melted when she walked down the stairs. Only she was there. She in that impenetrable veil and that insinuating voice.

"I don't…I don't know," he finally said astounded that he didn't know anything anymore. He rubbed his forehead. His whole face seemed to be on fire. He was sweating, hyperventilating.

"I really don't know," he repeated. "It was so long ago…."

Her swaying stopped and she dropped her hand. She turned a card.

"What is it?" he asked straining to see through the mist of candle light.

Her head tilted a little. She was like a doll, a broken doll. He imagined her with one eye open, staring, unblinking, the other eye down, broken, the thick doll eyelashes perfectly straight and the cut lid at the top of the sockets, a void of eye liner. He shivered.

"I don't know," she said in a suddenly chirpy, loving voice, a voice like a child telling of something pretty she found in a wood with an invisible friend and a magic bird. "I don't know," she said again, as if talking to herself, but he knew she did and he knew whom she addressed.

She looked right at him and his ears began ringing. His jaw clenched in a losing effort to stand up, to walk away, to be stronger than tears, but the bone became liquid. His head turned to sea waves surging in a tidal desire toward her knowing face, toward the terrifying white goddess moon behind that dark veil.

The border between terror and love evaporated. He sobbed uncontrollably. His body spasmed, bent him at the waist, and brought him to his knees. He tried to speak, but his sobs only deepened. No words of his, none from any mere human could swim across that oceanic gap. He was drowning, sinking down and floating up. He was almost gone.

"Shh," she whispered. "Be quiet. He's not here. You're not a little boy anymore."

He felt her hand on his back; its heat penetrated to the center of his heart. So warm. So loving. His breath slowed. He was in the water again. He tried to speak once more. His throat constricted. No breath. No voice. Whoever he had been before now surrendered completely into her world.

He collapsed to the floor and curled into a fetal position. His hands trembled violently, so violently he could not bring them to his face though he desperately wanted to hide his shame in those dark palms.

"Don't be ashamed," she sighed in a voice caught between love and despair. "These moments are the seeds of your future. Plant them deep. Shh. Shh." His sobbing slowly subsided as she slipped his head unto her lap and softly stroked the wetness of his hair.

"Shh. Let me tell you a story. Shh. Shh. There is always a time when we need new stories. A new story for a new life. That's all we are, you know? The stories we tell ourselves. The stories we believe. Shh. They are all made up. All of them, my love. The stories that make us cry, though, are the stories we want most to believe. Shh. Truth is in the tears. Shh. Shh."

***

Once upon a time there was a man, a man who wanted everything, everything in the world. He lived in an oasis, a paradise in the middle of a desert a thousand miles from the sea, a thousand miles from anywhere.

This man had a scar on his face that ran like a meat hook in a low arc from the bridge of his nose down his cheek to his mouth then over to the bottom of his left ear. It was two fingers wide and bone deep. A net of fine black wrinkles fanned from the edge of the scar across his cheek to his temple. That side of his face looked like a dark, fleshy veil sent from the land of djinn-bred dreams. The other side was handsome, as handsome as that of a prince of Egypt or even a god. But no one remembered ever seeing that side of his face for beauty is always invisible when it is coupled with horror.

His eyes were weak in the sunlight as were his father's. It was a condition his father attributed to a curse, a curse his father said was caused by the jealousy of the gods. Yet, he would offer no story to prove it, nor history or philosophy, and no one had the courage to ask him for the source of the curse. The father had a djinn's temper and his patience was less than a viper's. Any unwanted questions were answered with blows or worse. The son of the father had learned early not to look too closely at power, especially his own.

The man's eyes were always little more than slits; the squinting simply added further hardness to his cipher of a face, a black hieroglyph of need which was ever scanning the horizon for his next victim, his next conquest. And there was always a next victim, another conquest to be made. As I said, this man wanted everything; everything, and he came close to having it, but what he wanted most was to live on the sea.

He had never even seen the sea, but when he was a boy a traveler came upon his oasis lost and alone. The traveler said her horse had died and she asked for a drink from the oasis, but the boy, who had been put in charge of the oasis by his father, was a hard boy. He had been taught by the desert to give nothing but what could be taken back in equal or better measure.

"You should have chosen a better horse," the boy sneered.

"Yes," the woman said seriously. "Yes, I should have."

The boy stared at her, then said, "You are not Bedouin."

"No," answered the traveler in the boy's native tongue. "I come from a green, green land, far across the wide and tempestuous sea."

The traveler could tell by the expression on the boy's face that he did not understand what the word sea meant. The traveler smiled and nodded to the boy then waved her hands wide, gesturing to the endless expanse of sands that surrounded them.

"The sea is like the desert sands except it is so big that the desert itself would be like this oasis in the middle of the sea and the sea is made of water. Not sweet water like yours here in the oasis, but salt water, water that would only make you want more water if you tasted it. It is a water that never satisfies, yet it is so full of mystery that you can not help but want it more. Underneath its waves live untold numbers of fish and whales, seals, walruses and things we have not even seen, wondrous things, monstrous things. Animals, like birds and camels, but they live in the water, not on the land or in the air. It is a truly magical place beyond my power to describe, beyond the words of philosophers or even poets. It is the source of all life, of untold power, of riches unimaginable. Look, let me show you something."

The boy was absolutely entranced. He craned his neck as the traveler twisted around to reach into her canvas bag. She looked back at the boy and smiled playfully, but the boy wasn't looking at her. She was invisible now. All he wanted was the object that came from that enchanted place called the sea.

She took a deep breath. Then another to tease him. And then she held up a melon-sized object covered in a dark blue silk scarf.

"This," she whispered leaning close into the boy, "is something from the greatest ocean in the world. I found it when I traveled with my father many years ago, when I was a child no older than you. I keep it to remind me of my childhood and of home. There is only one in existence. There is none other like it. For this…" and she hesitated dramatically for a breath and watched as the boy's eyes grew wide with anticipation, "This is a spiked nautilus shell."

With a sudden laugh and an exaggerated magician-like pull on the scarf, the traveler thrust a marvelous shell high into the air and held it there glittering in the bright hot sun. Then, she slowly lowered her hand until it was inches from the boy's astonished face. The glistening, golden stripes of this treasure from beyond the boy's known world danced into his eyes and transfixed him.

It was more than anything he had ever imagined, as if magic itself materialized from the very air, becoming the transporting magic carpet, the wish-rich, golden lamp of the wondrous genie, the fountain of youth, and the lost mines of King Solomon. A present of deliciousness, of holy and forbidden mystery, something only spoken of by the mullahs or the traveling saints and dervishes, but it was more.

This wonder was not some heavy cloth of words, some thin cloud of music said to be the breath of angels. No imagination was needed here, no leap of faith or study of black scribbles. This magic could be held in his very own hands.

His heart sounded the thunder of Mohammed on the mountaintop. His breath raced like a wild stallion in battle with the infidel. He was the new prophet of the ages. He snatched the shell like the strike of a viper and was running into his tent before the woman finished her sentence. She smiled and followed the boy into the coolness of the red striped shelter.

The boy threw himself on a stack of pillows and began to cry. The woman frowned sadly and sat beside him. He lay there sobbing and sobbing, ignoring the gentle shushing of the woman. She did not reach out to him for she knew the customs of the land and what an insult it was for a woman to touch a man unbidden, even a man child.

"It's okay," said the traveler. "I, too, was once a child and was afraid to ask for what I wanted, thinking I would disappear into a dark land of shame when I was refused. But the fear is a greater enemy. Fear and pride have cost more lives than you can imagine. Shame is nothing beside those monsters."

The little boy looked up from his pillow. What was she talking about? He felt no shame. He was happy beyond words. He knew now that he could have everything. What was this crazy person saying? Who was this person? Did she think she would take his treasure from him? Was she a thief come to murder him and take away the magic of the world?

She was a djinn. A desert illusion that must be sent back to the bowels of hell.

His eyes were red. His face sneered his contempt. He had power and now he would use it.

The woman stiffened and turned her head sharply to the left to see what she thought was a man coming from the side of the tent. She swung around quickly but the boy was already at her. A knife slashed down but she managed to put her arm up. The knife barely penetrated and then ricocheted off her elbow. The woman grabbed the boy's hand and forced the knife back toward the boy.

The pommel of the knife was an elephant's head carved in ivory. Two tusks protruded beside its upraised snout. The tusks caught the boy at the bridge of the nose and then the woman pressed down and to the side. Blood shot out and the boy screamed. The woman let go and reached out to the boy with pity and terror in her eyes. The boy swung around with serpent quickness and slashed the woman across the throat.

Her eyes widened as her hands clasped at the mortal wound. Tears formed in her eyes and her knees collapsed. She fell forward and the boy stepped aside to watch her fall into the pillows next to the shell. Her blood flowed into the lip of the shell like a river into the sea.

The boy hovered silently over the woman holding the blood-drenched knife at his side, his rage still unspent. He studied her eyes, watching with a sneer as they dulled with every pulse of blood leaving her body. He bent just as the last spark left and whispered proudly, "It's mine."

She watched from the top of the tent. Watched as the knife left her throat and sprayed her blood across the pillows and unto the walls of the tent. Watched him fall to his knees and whisper that he was hers forever. Saw him suddenly drop the knife and cover his face as he ran screaming out into the desert. Floated down to look into her own beautiful white face. She had been lovely after all. Floated slowly back up to the top of the tent. Then with the speed of a comet-driven vortex, up she flew through the blue swirling heavens and into a honey-colored room carved in the side of a pale gray mountain. She listened to golden bells and read from a thick, leather-bound book. She read for centuries it seemed until a tall, thin man in a deep brown robe with a large cowl that shadowed his face came through the walls into her room. It was he she had seen in the tent. He had been her angel of death, sent to accompany her to this realm. He pointed to a page in the book with the image of the boy washing his bloody face in the oasis. The man leaned over from behind her and whispered something to her in a tongue she did not know but instantly understood. She floated gently back down to the earth, to the very oasis where she had died and entered silently into a dark chamber of the boy's beating heart.

She built a wall around herself and a moat around the wall. She placed sharks in the water and sentried her home with black tornadoes and red-eyed djinns with blue-skin and yellow fangs. Every night she let them loose into his dreams to torment him with their fearsome presence. Sometimes she appeared herself holding the nautilus before his scarred face, its curving belly open like an eye, an eye that would grow until it filled his terrified vision. In its blood-red center roared a black ocean. He could see its churning waves as if from a great distance. She slowly drew it back from him until she held it against her breast. As forbidding as it was, it was still the ocean and he had to have it, had to touch its thick liquid surface, smell its salty richness. When he reached out, as he always did, she let the demons loose.

The boy was hers now, though he did not know it, and she would bide her time. But she left a narrow niche open in the wall and drew two words in magic script. If ever he could find his way to the chamber and if he could read and then say the words, she would leave him. Years would pass before he ever approached the chamber.

Some say the boy was driven mad with the pain of the wound to his face. When he asked for everything he didn't expect all the pain, all the loneliness....

***

The veiled woman stopped speaking and her hand grew still on his forehead. He waited for a moment, expecting her to begin again, but the silence continued. He opened his eyes and started to speak, but held off. He turned his head a little toward her face and looked up. A tear fell from her cheek and landed on his. It burned.

He sat up and looked into her eyes. For once he could not see them. The veil's blackness deepened. Not even the light from the candles reflected from its voided surface. She was rock still. His body flooded with an uneasy excitement. He wanted to touch her face, to brush her cheek with the back of his hand, with his fingertips, lean closer and closer, whisper his secret thoughts and.... His hand rose as if following a mote of dust, slow motion tracking, a gentle swaying through a watery air.

"Do you know?" she asked in a single, sudden breath. The alien harshness of that voice crackled into his trance and he recoiled as if struck by a serpent.

"You want too much from this," she said more angrily, barely able to contain the rhythm of her breath. She stopped speaking and just breathed, hard. Her exhalation sounded like a lion after a kill—or perhaps before one. He almost stopped breathing. He waited and waited. And her breath slowed, but he could still hear the anger when she resumed.

"What you need are details," she said in a short clipped voice that eased as she continued. "People forget that. He forgot that. When you want everything you forget what matters. You forget the small things, the smells, the sounds, the soft hummings in a handful of meadow grass."

"The woman in the desert was so beautiful. I remember how she would crawl on her knees through the bushes in her garden when she was a child too young for school. The way her mother would brush her hair first with the boar bristle brush and then with her hand, smoothing it just so. Brush, hand, brush, hand. How beautiful and shining was her hair in the silver-backed mirror. How she would sit in the smooth wet sand at the ocean's edge, the shallow wavelets pushing at her back, she letting the gray silt flow through her funneling hands to make spiral towers on her reddening thighs. Ivory skin reddening. The black and white terns all around her chasing the fiddler crabs in a comical stop start, run, fast freeze, statue-still manner. Here. There. Look down. Cock your head. Move. Stop. Peck. Move. Stop."

"She holds the acorn-sized crabs in her cupped hands. Their bodies, frail golden glass, tickle her palms, the salt water so pungent in her face pressed close to the anxiously digging bodies. Her rubbery flesh is so much tougher than sand. She looks up dreamy-eyed and floating into the golden-tinged gray clouds. The clouds sliding around the sun setting over the islands to the west. Her hair dry, baked. The sand all through her hair like the tiniest of pearls glistening, a magic light on her smiling face. She was the summer sun."

"All these small, intimate moments, these memories so old, so fresh belong to the consciousness of the world. Yet a man who wants everything cannot afford such moments. Those memories that have no moral, no irony, no particular specialness...ordinary things. That's all they are. What wouldn't we give to have those moments again at the end of a life?"

She grew silent. The veil a void. His hand did not rise in temptation to see behind the veil. Whatever happened he would not violate her trust. The anger betrayed a vulnerability he did not expect in her. She was more fragile than he imagined and human enough, he knew, to hold vengeance close to her tender heart.

Yes, he was afraid of her, as afraid of her perhaps as he was inexplicably fascinated with her. More afraid because he might be in love with her. Hadn't she said fear and pride were enemies of humanity? He closed his eyes. He was afraid of her. Should he be ashamed of love and fear intertwined like this? Perhaps. He was not proud of it. But he would not deny it. He laid his head in her lap and waited for her to continue.

***

"After the murder," she said slowly, trying to find the rhythm she had before she had recounted the dead woman's childhood memories, "the boy wasted no time in his rise to power. His father returned from his travels with a war on his hands. The father hardly noticed his son's scar. The boy said something about a hunt. The father said he hoped it was worth it and then returned to his planning. The war involved a dispute with a local chieftain of Nubian descent.

The chieftain was a formidable fighter and relished a good battle above anything. Such an attitude meant the usual intrigue could not be employed. This put the father at a distinct disadvantage. The chieftain had already killed many of the father's best warriors and taken some strategic oases. The father was desperate. None of his counselors offered any advice he could trust. The boy listened intently to all that was said and then one day, despite his youth and the taboo against one his age speaking in council, he spoke.

"I can defeat him," the boy said matter of factly. The father looked at the boy and huffed before turning his back on his son. "I can do it easily. I know what he cannot refuse."

The father turned, sneering, but the boy knew he had his father's interest.

"Offer him your wife, my mother," the boy said thrusting his chin high.

The father flushed red in outrage. He started to draw his sword, but hesitated when the boy thrust his chin even higher. The father spit and slapped the boy hard across the face with the back of his fist, knocking him to the ground. The boy did not cry, didn't make a sound. He looked up at his father without a trace of feeling and repeated the offer.

"He will accept it, father."

"Your mother is dead, you fool. What is the matter with you? Did that hunting accident affect your mind as well as turn you into this camel ugly beast?"

"I will be the wife," the boy said. "A wife with a gift for our enemy."

The boy pulled the nautilus shell from beneath his robe.

"See the spikes?" the boy continued whispering and smiling devilishly while he pressed the tip of a spike into the tip of his left thumb. "Beautiful, aren't they? Imagine them pressed to a throat." He pressed a little harder and a bead of blood rolled into his palm.

"Why would he accept such a gift? What makes you think you would get past his inspection? He will inspect you."

"Yes, he will," the boy said with a smile the father had never seen before in his son. It was a smile he knew, however. He knew an assassin when he saw one.

"He will accept the bargain," the boy continued, "because he wants to shame you. He will take the bait and then he will try to betray you, but he will not have that pleasure. When he throws me to his guards I will fall to my knees and plead for your life. When he laughs I will rise and rip his throat out. Your men will be ready with arrows for his lieutenants. It's over in seconds."

The father stared at his son for a long time, not saying anything. Finally, he dismissed the boy with a sneer and wave of his hand, but the boy knew he had succeeded. After a brief talk with his council, the father called the boy back, agreed to the plan, and a meeting was set.

Three days later, under a banner of truce, the father, a small band of warriors, and the boy, draped in black from head to toe, approached the Nubian chieftain's encampment. The air was still and very dry. It seemed to the boy that every movement of the men, the horses, was like a cutting through stone, in stone. The boy loved it. Everything so big and obvious and inevitable. It was if he had seen it all before, seen it in the hard curvings of the nautilus shell. The victory was his before he could even discern which figure was the one whose throat he would slit.

His father and guards waited on their horses while the boy on horseback was lead by two escorts on foot to where the chieftain stood. The boy dismounted. Two of the chieftain's men walked up to the boy and grabbed him by either arm and held him. The chieftain walked up to the boy and reached out to lift the heavy black veils.

"Not here, please," the boy whispered. "In your tent I will show you everything."

"Yes, you will," the chieftain sneered. "And I will show you your cowardly husband's head."

"As you wish," the boy said coldly.

The chieftain turned and let loose a war cry. From beneath the sands two dozen men arose and arrows rained down on the boy's father. The father and most of his men fell dead instantly. The others spurred their horses away from the trap, but other Nubian warriors rose from the sands behind them and cut them down.

Distracted by his own cunning, the chieftain and the guards forgot the boy and the boy pulled the shell from beneath his robes. He tapped his victim on the shoulder, and when the grinning chieftain turned, the boy slashed open the man's throat with astonishing ease. The man fell to his knees, his hands limp by his sides. The boy pulled the chieftain's sword from its scabbard, lifted it above his head, and as the man fell forward, the sword flashed.

The boy calmly picked up the head and slowly turning brandished it before the startled warriors. Seconds before they had been filled with gloating victory but now they were paralyzed with an unspeakable fear.

"Bow down," the boy said with the thunder of heaven in his voice. "Bow before the power of the sea!"

They did more than bow. They prostrated themselves in the sand before this small black apparition who wielded the bleeding head of the most ferocious warrior any of them had ever known. They lay with their faces in the sand as he walked on their backs with the blood of their dead leader dripping over them. They lay trembling as the black beast ululated its victory song of the terrible power of the sea. They lay vowing in unison their undying allegiance to their new master.

From that moment on the boy spread his poisonous desire throughout the great desert lands laying waste to any who dared defy him. What he could not possess he destroyed. Years of war, treachery, and deceit made him the most powerful man in his world. He had gold, jewels, slaves, philosophers, and poets. He but asked and it was delivered. But still there were his dreams torturing him. Try as he may to imagine the sea, every time he crested a dream-dune black tornadoes and demon animals with mouths full of teeth barred his way. He asked magicians, herbalists, hermits, anyone who might know how to help him control his dreams. But he never told them why. He never once told anyone his desire. Something would not let him.

Nothing availed. His anger and ferocity grew with each passing day. His cruelty to those he conquered increased with every victory. And the dream demons became equally as fierce in their attacks upon him.

Still, closer and closer he came to the empire that lay on the coast. The empire between him and his greatest desire. In a vicious campaign his armies fought their way to the capital of the empire. He sent word through his emissaries to surrender or be killed to the last child.

Miraculously, the walled city offered its immediate willingness to bow to him. All he had to do was ride over a line of soft green hills and he would see the sea spread out before him with riches greater than any he could imagine.

All he had to do was ride over the green hills.

He arose before dawn on the appointed day of his triumphant entrance into the capital of the empire and mounted his favorite horse, a black stallion he had branded across the face to match his own scar. He dismissed his man-servant and rode by himself toward the hills.

As he neared the crest, he stopped. All these years. All the blood and gold that he had claimed as his own were as nothing to what lay ten strides away. He touched his scar gently, as a lover would caress the breast of the beloved. He trembled as he had the first time he had seen the shell.

He pulled the shell from the pouch he always carried with him. He raised it above his head. It would see the ocean before him, guide him into its mysteries. The blood-red sun broke over the crest. He spurred his horse forward.

This was her moment, the moment she had waited for. She entered the horse's heart with the thunder of Allah. The horse reared in terror and the shell fell from the man's hand. The horse reared again then collapsed as if it were made of water. The man leapt from the horse, but his foot caught in the stirrup and he fell face forward into the shell, its deadly spikes puncturing both his eyes.

He screamed and screamed in a pain that seared him to the core of his soul. The blood streamed from his useless eyes. It covered his hands as he pressed and pressed into his sockets. His ankle had been broken in the fall and he screamed louder when he tried to rise. He fell to his knees and began crawling forward. If he could not see his desire, he would hear it, taste it. He reached the crest and rolled down and down into a marshy pit.

He could hear the harsh cries of birds and a steady roar that pounded in his head. An acrid smell filled his lungs. Some hard-shelled thing crawled across his hand. He pulled himself backward. His skin suddenly burned. Biting sand fleas covered him. Gnats and mosquitoes buzzed in a black whirlwind about his face. His scar began to bleed. Then he heard the barking of dogs. Wild, snarling dogs coming his way.

He raised up on his knees.

"The sea! The sea!" he cried. He drew his sword, and pressing it to his heart, he fell upon it.

As his soul drifted up he turned to look to the sea, but there was nothing there. It was a white void trembling with heat. From its subtle waves he saw the woman he had murdered floating toward him. In her hands she carried the nautilus shell still dripping with his blood.

"This was my heart," she said softly.

"I did not want your heart," he said. "All I ever wanted was the sea."

"It was not yours for the taking. Do you know why you did not get to see the ocean?"

"Yes. Yes, I do," he said turning from her, but she was there in front of him when he looked up again.

"Why?"

"Because I didn't ask you," he replied.

"Yes. And why was that?"

"Because I was afraid you would deny me."

"Why?"

"Because if I had such a treasure I would not give it away."

"I was dying of thirst," she said.

"So was I."

She smiled sadly and held the shell toward him. He reached for it tenderly.

"You didn't want the sea," she said. "What you wanted was love. And love is always mixed with fear. You just took the fear and disappeared. Now you cannot even ask for forgiveness."

He stared at her as he had that first day. But this time she turned and was gone. He didn't move. He stood there with his hand outstretched and waited and waited. But the whiteness never varied. Its waves of heat spread out into infinity and slowly, as slow as a rock turns to sand, the man faded into nothingness. And so the story ends.

***

He trembled in the silence of the room. A sudden cold wind blew through the open window and the candles went out. He muffled a cry and she stroked his cheek.

"Shh, my darling. It's just the wind. Remember? It always comes this time of night. See the moonlight on the floor? It's time. You are almost ready for your swim."

"I'm afraid," he stuttered. "I…I don't understand why I'm so afraid."

"You know what you want, don't you?"

"Yes. Yes, I do."

"Good."

"But why am I afraid? That was so many years ago. He wouldn't have really let me drown. He loved me. He just wanted me to be the best. I wasn't ready. He really wouldn't have let me drown. My father loved me."

She said nothing as she gently stroked his hair, then she bent down and kissed his forehead.

"To want everything is to treasure nothing," she whispered. "You know what to treasure. In treasuring there is fear. Forgive yourself for being afraid of what you want. Forgive him for not being everything to you. I did. You can figure out the rest for yourself. It is time for me to go."

"No, not yet," he said rising up. But she was gone. He looked to the tower stairs but the door was already shut. He still had so many questions. What did she mean? Who did she forgive? Was she the woman with the shell? Was he that man…?

"Who am I?" he whispered.

The wind died down and he re-lit the candles and stared at the dancing light. He breathed slowly, steadily, waiting for something to change. He waited and waited and then blew the candles out. She would be waiting for him tomorrow night as she always waited. Perhaps, she would tell him what he wanted to know. Perhaps not. But now, it was time.

He walked down to the sea and watched the waves crawl closer toward him. He waited for the fear to go away. It didn't, but he closed his eyes, saw her face, and walked slowly into the dark waters.

The Valley of Ashes

No candles lit the room when he walked in. Only the dim light of the cloudy night sky washed through the curtainless windows. The door to the tower was open, so he knew she was there. Perhaps she waited in the shadows just a few steps up the stairs.

When the moon hid, she didn't like to come down. He felt a little guilty on those days, drawing her into his world. But his soul hungered and, besides, she needed his desire as much as he needed her reflection. At least that was what he told himself, what he had to believe.

He stood for a moment looking through the open window to the west. The long, low rolling meadow stretched out to the dark line of distant trees, a mix of oak, elm, birch, a linden or two. Just beyond them lay the sea, a flat shimmering silver, tarnished by the will-o-the-wisp absences of the teasing moon. He smiled at that description. Melancholia can be so comforting—self-pity is such an accessible pacifier.

After a few moments, he turned away from the window and sat at the table waiting for her to come into the room. He didn't want to rush her. He was practicing humility. She was the teacher. It was hers to speak when she was ready. He would wait patiently.

He sat erect with his hands in his lap, eyes open, lips closed. But meditation didn't mediate for him as it had in his youth. He began picking at his nails, then slowly rocked back and forth silently singing a maudlin song he'd been playing over and over in his study at home.

He closed his eyes and pictured himself walking through the meadow toward the line of trees and the tarnished sea. At the edge of the trees he stopped.

Something waited there in the dark. Something he didn't want to meet.

He opened his eyes.

She was sitting at the table, the cards spread out before her.

"You are so pitifully self-indulgent," she sighed, lighting the fourth candle.

"Why do you say that?" he asked, trying not to blink too much. How long had he been tranced, he wondered? He could feel her knowing smile. She somehow knew about the woods.

She turned her head to look out the window. A break in the clouds let a pool of moonlight play on the tops of the trees. She lifted her chin a little as if absorbing its pale energy.

"Why do you want my stories?" she pressed without looking at him.

He hesitated.

"I…I want them," he stuttered, "because I…."

He shrugged. He was too embarrassed to answer, too uncomfortable. Very uncomfortable. She knew about the woods. What else did she know?

He covered his face with his hands. His breath pulsed short and fast. He knew the answer.

"I want them," he continued, steady, strong, but still with his face covered, his fingertips tapping his forehead. "I want them because…they have a wisdom…a beauty. They have what I don't have, what I…."

He released his face and pressed his hands to his lips silently pleading with her for a reprieve. She was still looking out the window.

He wanted to jump up and run, run as far away from her as he could, back through time, back to when he did not know her, to a place where he'd never known her.

She turned to face him, slowly, as if she were a mechanical doll. "You're hungry for a sop. A wisdom and beauty sop, you know?" she said, shaking her head flatly, a thin smile not quite perceptible. "Why are mine different than what you could find…anywhere? Out there in those woods? Wading in the waves of that tarnished sea? Wisdom lies there, too."

"I do not know them like I know you," he shot back, straining not to bite the words in two, desperate to find a respectable line of escape.

"You don't know me. You only know a woman who sits at a table in candlelight and tells you stories. The stories are not me."

"Who are you, then?"

She laughed. "That's cruel, don't you think? Don't answer. Cruelty's just another form of indulgence. You are so steeped in it I wonder how you ever found me at all? Stop talking. You need to learn to listen."

"But talking is a way to bridge the gap, to bridge the silences that separate us." He had something with that, he thought, something he could cling to, a philosophy.

"Stop talking. Perhaps then you'll see bridges everywhere and not just gaps to feed that insatiable word hole."

"Yes," he said, surrendering. "I know. How do I do that?"

"Stop talking. Listen. You know you are not special? You are unique. But not special. There is a difference. You think words are special, but you're wrong. Stop talking and learn to hear your own voice."

He opened his mouth to speak, but she held a finger to his lips and said, "Shh."

"Close your eyes again," she whispered. "See the woods? You see them? Stop talking to them. I can hear you talking to them, analyzing them, reducing them. Stop seeing their darkness and listen to their darkness."

"Your fears about them, about yourself, are only lies. The lies have hidden the light that lives in those fears. The darkness is the fear story you tell yourself. Free the light hidden in the story. Free the darkness to be the womb of all that is, not just the focus of your doubts. Hear the voice beyond the stories, the breath of the story. Shh. Don't scowl. I will tell you a story. I will indulge you in the paradox. Shh. Listen."

***

Once upon a time there was an ugly, old, hunchbacked man who lived in a forest of talking trees. It was a most marvelous place, as you can well imagine, full of dancing leaves and swaying limbs and the strangest, most beautiful of songs. But this man could not appreciate this wonder because, for one thing, he was stone deaf.

For another, it was just a terribly windy forest where branches constantly slapped at his face and leaves blurred the mark for his chopping ax. What he needed was firewood, not leafy literature or resinous wisdom from an enchanted forest.

As far as he was concerned the trees were nothing but a nuisance, a nuisance and a curse. Not only did they hamper his profession, but they hindered his view of the surrounding blue mountains and the distant silver sea. Worse, they obscured his view of the flights of his beloved eagles.

It was his singular pleasure to watch the sea eagles soar down from their high aeries. He thrilled in their hunts on the cold, wild rivers near his hut or around the teeming marshes close to the sea lying at the foot of the mountains.

Often, the most heart-stopping part of an eagle's dive would be cut from view by the suddenly swaying trees. Such a thing would throw the old man into a rage that could last days. He stormed red-eyed and puffing through the forest swinging his ax in a blind fury, spending himself against the hated wood until he collapsed in unfulfilled exhaustion.

Yet such intense hatred did not spring from thwarted pleasure alone. There was a deeper reason. The trees tormented him with memories he'd rather have lost. He had been able to put up with them for years, but he was getting old and intolerant.

So one morning, after a night recovering from one of his fits, the ugly, old, hunchbacked man woke up determined there would be an end to it. He would cut down all the trees. All of them. None would be spared.

He reasoned there would be enough firewood to last his lifetime. The rest he could sell to the villagers in the mountains and on the coast. Or when he grew tired he would just let the logs rot where they fell. It was no matter to him. The trees would be gone and his days of torment would be at an end.

He set about his task with a determination he had not known since his youth. He made very good progress for a month or two, but after awhile not even his rage sufficed and he grew tired. True, he told himself, he had made a good start. Half a year of hard, honest work from dawn until dusk had yielded a mountain of firewood for him and more than enough to sell to the villagers. Still there were trees, and he wanted none.

He sat all day on a stump, his chin resting on an ax handle, thinking on what to do, but nothing came to him. He finally went to bed and as he pulled his covers up to his chin he watched the last rays of the sun dance on the highest peak of his blue mountains.

A slow smile broke out across his leathery face as he mouthed the word, 'Fire.' He turned on his side, curled his legs to his chest and hugged them. He closed his eyes triumphantly and instantly fell into a long dreamless sleep.

The next morning the ugly, old, hunchbacked man woke up refreshed. He had breakfast of cold mush and onions, performed his morning chores quickly but with care, then happily set about his task of setting the forest afire.

He threw a small torch every five paces as he walked along the edge of the forest. The winds blew in from the sea as they always did that time of the morning. They were stronger than usual and fanned the flames deep into the forest with a quickness that delighted the old man.

More than satisfied with his work, he walked back to his hut, sat on a stump and watched the flames and smoke rise like a new sky into the new morning.

The forest burned for days and days and into weeks. But the smoke did not dissipate. It became an immovable wall that waited and waited until the last tree breathed itself into soft white ash. Then in a great stunning roar it let itself loose on the world.

Like an army of white-hot stars the smoke poured down the valley. It crossed the mountains into the helpless lands in its path and screamed toward a dark and distant kingdom lying over the sea.

The voices of the forest rode inside the smoke. And as it had done everywhere the smoke of voices passed, when it entered the kingdom across the sea, the voices filled the air with their torment and their sadness, their anger, their laughter and joy, their unspeakable wonder.

But everyone touched by the smoke trembled with dread and confusion. They heard no joy, no wonder in those mysterious clouds. They heard and saw only monsters.

Slowly people began to die in the madness of the hideous smoke.

The ruler of the kingdom was troubled beyond measure. Nothing his magicians, priests, or scientists tried could disperse the smoke. The people clamored for a champion. But the king had no champion. He himself was too frail. His only remaining son hated him.

The king's rank meant nothing to the smoke, a smoke which relentlessly reminded him that all his sorrows stemmed from his own dark conflicts.

A year before the smoke entered the kingdom a war had begun with an old and terrible enemy. The youngest prince had refused to take up the king's sword to instead become a poet. His indulgent father let the boy have his way for he held tender feelings for the boy's dead mother. But as the war went badly the people began to resent the indulgences of kings for no one indulged the needs of the people. Their wants went unanswered as the war took more and more of the kingdom's treasure. Despite the grumbling and wicked gossip, the father left the boy alone.

Then one pale autumn morning, the king's older sons and thousands of his soldiers fell in a bloody slaughter. The king lost his lands across the sea and his people began speaking of rebellion.

Grief-stricken and humiliated, the king flew into a rage when the boy poet read his father a lament he'd written about the war. The king attacked and beat his son so severely that blood burst from the boy's ears and the boy went deaf.

The boy ran to a small room at the top of the castle keep's tallest tower and refused to come out. Night after night his mournful wails of shame echoed out over the castle grounds.

The people merely shook their heads in disgust. The king fell into an embittered self-loathing broken only by the curse of the smoke.

The people began to blame the prince for the curse. If the king would find no champion then they demanded the deaf coward be burned at the stake. Only a royal sacrifice, a blood messenger from the kingdom's divinities could assuage the voices that lived in the smoke.

The king would have nothing to do with such a plan. He knew the smoke was killing him and he knew that with his death, his only remaining son could not escape the vengeance of the people.

The king called the prince from his tower and gathered together the court and prominent citizens. He announced that he had seen in a vision the cause of the smoke. The people were correct: a champion was needed. He had seen in this vision a great dragon tormenting a princess across the sea. It was the breath of the dragon that was causing this torment. The lady was resisting the dragon's will and so it was up to the prince to honor her resistance and go forth and slay the dragon. Thus there would be an end to the curse and a royal union as well.

He presented his son an ancient sword boasting a gold handle encrusted in diamonds and with a blade of double-forged Damascene steel. The king informed his son that if it were a dragon causing the plague of smoke and the tormenting voices, then the sure bite of the royal tooth would end its strangling reign of terror.

Everyone in the throne room heard that 'if.' They knew there were no other options this time. The prince must take up the sword. He must try to save the kingdom and restore his family's honor. The boy certainly understood. He understood it all.

The king kissed his son for the last time. He knew in the formal setting the boy would not refuse his gesture. The prince received the kiss, but refused the eyes that asked for forgiveness. The boy turned from the father and let him watch as he stiffly walked back down the long red carpet with the angry eyes of the court burning into his back.

The entire court knew the king's story was a lie, but he was the king. What could they do? Still, everyone knew, dragon or no, the prince would never return.

The next morning the boy wrapped his face and his horse's face in a sheer black veil fitted with clear glass. Only his father, carried in a litter by four silent guards, came out to see him off. The rest of the kingdom stayed indoors and prayed for the prince's death.

The prince knelt before his father. The king softly touched the boy's hair. He let his hand rest there for a moment. His hand slipped gently toward the boy's left ear. The prince looked up, his face grown suddenly hard beneath the veil. The king winced. He would not see forgiveness.

He signaled to his guards to lift him in the litter and return to the keep. He raised his hand again and the guards stopped. He started to say something to his son, but he could not. He only coughed and rubbed his eyes and finally barked to the guards to take him back to the keep.

The prince remained kneeling until his father was completely gone. He then stood and walked to the horse. He stroked the horse's face for a few moments as if it were the face of a child. A shaking snuffle from the horse ended the prince's reverie and he frowned, quickly jumped on the horse and spurred it forward. He disappeared into the enveloping smoke as if he had never been there.

A day later, a royal boat took him across the sea. When he landed, the prince traveled directly east following the smoke toward the dying forest. Almost immediately the smoke grew thicker. It was difficult to breathe even through the veil. His horse tired quickly and they made little progress.

Each day the air became colder. A freezing rain set in. In the mornings he pulled icicles from his bark-hard clothing. When he touched his hair the locks fell off like brittle leaves.

Four weeks into the journey it began to snow. His mouth set in a hard frown, he rode forward into the blinding blizzard. He rode and rode and rode, sunrise to sundown, day after day, until finally he arrived in the blasted valley where the smoke of the talking trees still swirled up from the burning earth.

It was nightfall. He was barely alive, but he was in the mouth of the cursed valley. He sniffed the air for sulfur, but he really didn't expect to find such a beast. All he smelled was his own foul breath.

He sighed. Whatever lived in the valley could wait until morning. He was tired beyond fear. He dismounted and at once his horse fell dead. He said nothing. His face registered nothing. There was nothing to do for the dead, he thought.

Nothing to do for the dead, so he cut open the horse's belly and crawled into it.

When he awoke the valley seemed shrouded in a deep snow with the air clearer than it had been in days, though still quite misty. But something was moving in the valley. Something big. He crouched behind the horse and shaded his eyes. Slowly the vision came into focus. It chilled every chamber of his heart.

Solid mists of smoke curled angrily into the sky like sharp, frigid fingers, column upon column like an endless army of mile-high giants. Each swirling mast of cloud held a human face contorted in pain, burning in a white flame, their skins melting, blood boiling; their souls screaming in eternal agony.

The prince looked away. He splashed some of the horse's blood on his face. This was madness, a dream. It couldn't be real. He wanted something real. Something had to be done. He had to wake up if this were a dream. He had to act as if this were real. He had to move.

"Act and the madness disappears," he said aloud.

He pulled out his sword, held it pointed straight up, stared at its gleaming edges. But his hand trembled uncontrollably. The weight of the sword was immense, debilitating. He struggled desperately to hold it up.

His head ached. He felt woozy. His breathing slowed then sped up rapidly. The visions pummeled him, faces like fists….

He swung at the empty mists.

Whose faces…? What do they want? How could he take a steel sword to a cloud? How could ghosts feel steel? He could swing forever and all he would achieve would be a slow rusting. He could hide forever….

"What good a rusty sword?" he whispered.

He pressed the sword point to his throat.

"Yes, that's it. Put away the sword, put it where…. Dream. Sleep with the brothers…in the…fields of…white…shame. The gods live in the stars…are dead. Put the sword here…."

"No! Wake up!"

He took a deep breath. The air was sharply cold, cutting into his nostrils and into his lungs. He gritted his teeth and slowly, deliberately brought his full attentive gaze onto the scene before him. The madness faded. Behind the veil, his eyes widened in proud anger. With a fierce, bone-bled cry he stood and turned and turned, faster and faster, spinning and spinning, roaring as he flung the sword deep into the blasted valley.

And then he waited for the recoil. Waited. Waited. Each breath defiant in its slow deliberateness.

One.

Two.

Three.

Four.

Nothing. The rank mists swallowed his action as if it were no more than the dying breath of a rose.

Then it was there.

His legs quavered. He could feel it rising from the earth through his body, but he didn't fight it. He let it shake its way up his body and into his jaw, into his head…and out.

No matter the consequence, he would not yield the ground.

He stood staring anxiously into the bright, silent maws of the malevolent landscape waiting for a movement, some other reaction from the hellish white vortices. Their intelligence, their presence surrounded him, shot through him. Yet it was only white absence.

Nothing.

They would present no force for him to face. There would be no eye to outstare, no strength of arms to best. No mind to outwit.

Hopeless, he fell to his knees and wept uncontrollably. He wept until his body collapsed and he slept like a stone in a forgetful river.

When he opened his eyes she was there. She was unspeakably beautiful. She wore a long, flowing white gown in a textured pattern of intertwined leaves and vines with a scattering of small, delicate plum blossoms splashed across her breasts like a wave of stars dropped by a careless god. On her feet were soft, white, elk skin slippers. Ice white hair fell in loose curls to her pearl white shoulders. Even her lips and cheeks were but a shade darker than her ivory throat.

She was utterly white except for her eyes. White ashes and red eyes. Red fire eyes. A dream, he thought. The spirit of the forest. The smoke of a dying world. Death.

Her hands stretched toward him. Yet, there was no movement of the hands from her side. They were just suddenly extended. It was as if time were making small leaps. Like a fire.

Like the gaps in a fire, he thought.

There is no fire in a spot and then there is. A clear heat followed by blue flame. Instantaneously there, gone, there. Her hands were before him like a sudden flame.

There was a white box. A wooden white box. Small. A jewelry box. Closed. Open. Something in it. White. Gold. Voices. Visions. A leap of flame. A coffin. An old man asleep. A gap. Children gathering firewood in a meadow along the edge of a wood. Strange song from the deeper part of the wood. Something dangerous waiting for them. Something in the box.

There. Rolling out before him, clearer than any dream, he saw a man's life, the life of the man who would grow up to burn down the most magical of all forests. He saw him as a boy playing with friends at the end of a summer's day....

An old man, bent and raggedy, steps from behind a dark, gnarled tree. He grabs the young boy, hits him over the head with a cudgel, and drags him into the darkness of the wood. The boy's friends run away, screaming. Night falls quickly. The boy is led to a small, one room cabin. Cold, dark. Only moonlight plays across the dirt floor. A coffin stands in the corner.

The boy is inside now, feeling blows to the coffin. The old man half-blind and raging at the kidnapped boy locked in the coffin. How was he to know the boy was deaf? He needed a servant, anyway. He had no money. What was he to do? It didn't matter what the voices in the forest said. They weren't half-blind. They got what they needed without any struggle. They stole from the earth, from the air, from the sun! He had a right! How different was what he did? It was there for the taking. Damn the trees. Who were they to say what was necessary for a man to live?

Ever since he'd cut down the old oak by the salmon pool all the other trees did was curse him anyway. But he made a good coffin of it. Covered the inside with the bitter tar to shut it up. The old oak's voice would at last be silent. And now that's where the boy would stay until he was broken, until he knew who was master and who servant. This was the wisdom of hard times. The trees would have to accept that. This was the boy he had chosen.

The boy struggled for the first few days. He wanted to hate the old man. But he didn't know him well enough. Not yet.

He watched for him from the corner of his eye. Though he was half-blind, the old man had the hearing of a cat and the boy soon gave up trying to escape from the old man's service.

What he wanted most was to escape the blows.

The old man laughed like a jackal each time he caught the boy off guard. It was his version of cat and mouse, a game of tag. But it was a cruel hunting game in the boy's eyes.

Once the boy picked up a piece of firewood and lunged at the old man, but the old man was quick and the beating that followed left the boy with a broken nose and a broken right shoulder that never healed properly.

The broken shoulder made the whip-thin boy appear even more hunchbacked. And because his left eye was stronger than his right his head was always turned slightly to the right in constant vigilance. With the crooked nose and sidewards glancing, the boy looked like a twisted scrub oak made human, made almost human.

There was one standing mirror in the cabin. When the old man was not around, the boy would stare into the mirror, studying his twisted shape until he imagined wings growing from his shoulders and a beak sprouting from his long, broken nose. He became an eagle flying through the blue, open sky heading toward his mountain aerie. In his claws he held a giant salmon plucked from the stream that ran clear and cold down by the fields. The salmon's flesh tasted so tender and sweet, but in the boy's vision its head was the old man's head. The boy-eagle tore the head off with his razor sharp beak and tossed it into the gully for the vultures to pick at.

As month after month passed, the boy grew more distant, fled deeper into his world of clouds and eagles. The old man unrelentingly threw him into the coffin and slammed its lid.

The boy had learned nothing, the old man thought. There was so much to teach him, but it is true: You can't teach anyone anything. They can only choose to learn. He felt sorry for the boy. That's why he kept him. What else would the world do with an ugly boy who wouldn't listen? He'd done what the voices had told him to do. The boy needed the discipline. It was hard. He knew that. But he himself had learned. He had. He really had.

The old man would open the coffin and stare at the sleeping boy. He wanted it to work. Life was hard, but all the tests were passable. We were made for this life so nothing was impossible for us. All we needed was the discipline to learn. Discipline.

As he stared at the boy, at the frailty of the young, hunchbacked boy, he remembered his own childhood. He remembered the way he had felt as a boy when he was taken and his breath would catch him in the throat. He forced it back down with a cough, a tightening of the jaw, and a twist of his thin lips. Not pity, he'd tell himself. No, not pity. Discipline was what the boy needed. He'd brush the boy's hair from the eyes, smooth it and tuck it behind the boy's ears. Discipline, he'd say, and shut the lid down again.

Inside the coffin, the boy never stirred. As he dreamed, the spirit of the chopped down oak, father of the talking trees, spoke to him, visited him with scenes of unimaginable beauty. It sang of a wisdom that reached from deep inside the earth itself, into the sun that burned as brightly inside the earth as the one that burned in heaven. It tried to bring that wisdom to the golden, burning heart of the boy, bring it through the thick black mantle of angry bitterness the boy had built around his heart to absorb the daily pain and torture the old man visited upon him.

But the tar inside the coffin kept the dreams contained. The wisdom of the oak could not leave the coffin except through the human heart. The boy gradually began to stay out in the fields at the edge of the woods. He stared at the trees and seemed, to the old man, to be studying the movement of the leaves. The boy began to gather fallen limbs instead of chopping down trees for firewood.

The old man would not let such things pass. He knew the tricks of the coffin and everyday he beat the boy harder, made him do senseless chores, and rewarded him with more blows. Whatever the boy did it wasn't good enough or fast enough or done to the old man's changing standards. The mantle over the boy's heart grew thicker. Every day the sun that had been the core of his heart became emptier. The songs of the oak grew louder, the dreams more vivid. But they stuck in the tar and the boy slowly forgot them.

He even flinched less around the old man. The blows from those gnarled fists meant nothing to him. The old man took to beating him with tar-covered oak staffs. Deeper and deeper the boy fell into the bitter hole where his heart had been. No longer would the old man have to pull the boy into the coffin. The boy climbed into the coffin and closed the lid on himself.

The old man smiled. He had won.

One day the old man woke the boy and gestured for him to follow. He was going to take him to a place the boy had never been, a secret place, the old man said. The boy could read lips, but he wondered why the old man continued to jaw at him after he turned his back. He knew the old man did because of the hand gestures. He hated those meaningless movements. Hated it in the old man; hated it in the trees. They were mocking him as far as he could tell. He turned to go outside, but stopped when the old man stomped the floor.

"This way, boy," the old man lipped. He shuffled to the standing mirror, picked it up, and leaned it against the blocked window next to the coffin. He knelt on the floor and lifted some boards. A wet, sickly smell emanated from the ground, a swampy stench of decay.

"Worms," the old man said out of the side of his mouth as he stretched out on the floor. He was breathing heavily. "Nightcrawlers still down there. I meant to take you fishing. Catch some big ones. Feed 'em to the eagles. But I could tell you wouldn't like it."

The old man reached into the narrow gap of the floor boards grunting and grimacing as he patted the warm, worm-rich earth, but his face relaxed into a smile as he pulled out a long narrow box, his fingers dripping with humus and worm blood.

"This. This is what it was all about," the old man insisted as he pulled the dirty box up beside him. He didn't rise from the floor, but lay beside the box like an excited little boy studying a long-promised present finally arrived. He lay there smiling, stroking the box, knocking off dirt and cobwebs as he spoke, flicking a startled spider with a yellow, hard-bitten nail.

"You didn't understand," he huffed as if lifting the box was the hardest work he had done in years. "You didn't understand at first, but you will now. I was the same way. But it was worth it. I came to understand that it was worth it. No pity. Discipline. No tears. No tears. All that.... I can have it. I can have what I waited for."

His voice trailed off for the last few words and then he stopped speaking altogether. His demeanor completely changed. He had been acting like an excited little boy, but within a breath he had become a tired, confused old man, a very old man. He shook his head a little as if shaking off a spider that might have crawled into his hair. His eyes glazed for a moment and then widened. He pushed the box away and stood up.

"Is there something there? You see something, don't you? Kill it. Kill it for me, boy."

The urgency in the old man's voice didn't have its desired effect. The boy stood there unmoved as the old man's words grew louder and more shrill. The boy smiled as he watched the old man stomping up and down and pointing at the box screaming out commands. The old man seemed to have forgotten that the boy was deaf.

Whatever the old man was saying it was clear he was frightened. A smile slowly washed across the boy's face. Something was going to happen today. Something terrible. Something deliciously terrible.

The old man backed himself into the wall. He raised his chin and sniffed the air desperately.

"Do you smell it?" the old man screeched. "That's my life, boy. Burning. Burnt. Open it. Quick. Do you smell it? All those years?"

Why was the old man frightened of a box, the boy wondered. No matter, he concluded. The fear needed no explanation, only guidance.

A fist-sized black and red spider disturbed by the commotion in its underground world scurried across the top of the box. The old man noticed the movement. It was the box coming to take its revenge. He screamed. And he screamed again. He took in a breath for a third time and held it, held it with his mouth open. His thin lips quivered like a fish gasping for watery air, silent in the dryness and alone in the blankness of all those waiting years, all those years he had told himself to have no pity, to wait.

The boy stared at the fish-mouthed old man and he felt the rush of a wind, an ancient wind pressing him down, down and away. It passed through him in an instant and in its passing left his soul heavy, so heavy that it had no choice but to fall. Down and away in a trance.

The boy slowly raised his right hand and curled the fingers tighter and tighter into a bloodless fist. He pointed a gaunt, crooked index finger at the spider and then he laughed, a stiff, contorted laugh that lacked even the joy of spite. He was laughing at his own terror, belittling his own fears; fears felt because of a broken old man, an old foul fish not even fit for an eagle's claw come down on an ancient wind.

His arm fully extended, he wanted to lift it higher and turn. He wanted to point at the old man. Point and laugh. Point and rage and claw out the old man's cloudy grey eyes. Spy him from above and bring his talons into his filthy flesh, into that hated, frightened face and make him feel the pain and terror of his captivity.

In his mind he flew into a thunderstorm so fierce it frightened the gods. But his body wouldn't move. He realized he, too, stood open mouthed pointing at the air like a mad man frozen in time.

The spider crawled across the top of the box and back into the hole. The old man was released from his trance and slammed his fist down where the spider had slipped over the side. He slammed it again and again until the boy saw blood.

"See?" the old man bellowed. "See what you've done, you ungrateful boy?"

He picked up the box and hurried toward the door stopping only long enough to kick over the mirror and stomp the shattered glass. The boy saw nothing now. He hid beyond even where eagles live and die.

The old man turned back at the threshold of the hut and walked back to the still petrified boy. He looked deep into the boy's eyes. They were dull, glazed as if cataracts had suddenly formed in that very instant, the instant when the boy's soul froze.

"You're colder than I ever was," the old man sneered when the boy's eyes shifted to gaze back. The old man snorted contemptuously and spit in the boy's face, turned around and left.

"Cold," the boy thought from a space beyond the furthest star's black rim, 'I'll show you cold, old man."

The boy walked mechanically outside to the dilapidated shed, grabbed an ax from the wall, and followed the old man into the forest. In less than an hour he found him down by the shallows of a salmon river.

Several eagles circled low in the hazy sky, waiting for a salmon to slither into the rocky channels. One stood on a stump pulling the entrails from a still squirming victim.

The old man sat close by the water with the box, still unopened, cradled in his arms. He rocked slowly back and forth humming a lullaby.

He looked up only to see the ax come down.

***

The flash of steel and bright spray of dark blood jerked the prince away from the smoky vision and his sword fell to the ground. He stared wide-eyed at it for a moment expecting it to turn into a snake. Hadn't he thrown the sword into the valley? What dream was this?

Then he remembered where he was, why he was there.

He stopped breathing.

Slowly, he looked up. He almost hoped she would be gone, but she stood there, statue-still and silent and terrifyingly beautiful. The word "breathe" slipped into his mind as if in a language and from a time ages past. The prince breathed and he dropped his gaze to the sword. He again saw the ax come down. Heard the stifled scream and saw the blood. He watched in the vision as an eagle tugged at a sinew of a withered hand fallen into a stream.

"What...what happened to him?" the prince stuttered in his thoughts. "It was him, wasn't it? It was his story? Is he...buried in the ashes of this fire...this fire he set?"

The woman didn't answer. Not so much as a hair moved in the wind that whipped about them.

The prince peered down at the brightly jeweled sword his father had given him so long before. It lay in the ashes as if in a grave. The prince could not stoop to pick it up. Every fiber in his body denied his downward movement. He sat there and sat there; his thoughts black glue filling his soul. He sat through the windstorm, through the fall of that night and the next and the next. The wind never abated, but the ashes only grew thicker around him.

Yet the sword remained visible, the sword he had refused, had taken finally as a gesture of resignation. He watched as it slowly rusted away to nothingness.

The woman in white never moved. She held the box in her arms, waiting. The prince sat encrusted in white ash. He felt his body disintegrating. Move, he told himself. All he had to do was bend a little. Bend a little and extend his hand. Pick up the sword and whatever this was, whatever madness this was, would evaporate. All he had to do was pick up the sword. All he had to do was take a step forward and bend.

He couldn't do it. Tears welled in his eyes, rolled down his face, and dried in the wind.

Move. All he had to do. All he had to do. All he had to do.

He closed his eyes and said, "Let the darkness come."

The woman extended her arms. The prince felt the movement and his eyes fluttered open. Dimly through the swirling ash an eagle landed on the box, spread its wings and screeched. The prince did not hear the harshness of the call, but its mouth seemed the gateway to hell, its bright red tongue the flames of the prince's shame. It screeched again, and for a moment the prince saw the boy's face wrenched in anger as the ax came down.

The eagle screeched again and the prince's back straightened, his chest expanded with a deep in-breath of the freezing air.

It screeched again and the ashes on the prince's body began to crumble. The eagle slapped its wings against the wind and the ashes flew from the boy's body. The prince witnessed the whole scene as from a distance. It felt as if the icy moon had exploded and revealed a blazing sun.

He stood straight up, pulled by the force of the vision. With a slow deliberate movement, he yanked off the veil and dropped it calmly into the ashes. He stared deeply into her eyes. He took one step, leaned over, picked up the sword without looking at it, and pressed it flat against his thigh.

"My father is dead," he said to the woman.

"Yes," she whispered.

"He forgave me. He forgave me everything."

"Yes."

"I can hear," the prince weakly smiled.

"Yes," the woman answered. "Yes, you can hear and you can tell what you have seen, the stories, and of what has been lost. You speak for them now. All of them, all of this."

"What's in the box?" the prince asked.

"What was lost by the hunchback, by the old man. What has been lost by everyone who has taken the gift of a wound and squandered its hidden treasure."

"Will it…can it ever come back?"

"It is too late for some. Who knows your future?" she answered, her eyes for the first time softening as she looked not through but into the prince. "Though you now know the gift your father gave you when he wounded you, you will never be shiny and new again. There is the rust and that is your own light and grace. It will remind you that every love has its cost."

She turned from him and raised the box into the air. The eagle flew straight up then dropped into a steep dive. The woman released the box. The eagle caught it and slowly lifted it into the sky. The prince and the woman watched silently as the boy and his dream disappeared into the breaking clouds.

The woman took a few steps and stopped. She looked back over her shoulder at the prince. He gently sheathed the rusty sword and without a word followed her into the swirling mists unafraid, forgiving.

***

The woman in the tower fell silent. He could feel her still sitting beside him, but he knew she was looking out the window, into the woods. A few moments passed as they both listened to the winds stir in the distant trees. He heard her rise from the chair. He took a deep breath. He knew what was in the woods. He had to tell her.

"No," she whispered. "Stay quiet, stay with the dark for awhile."

"Yes," he replied.

When he finally opened his eyes the candles were out, the table cleared. The tower door was closed. The floor sparkled with milky moonlight. The clouds, too, had disappeared. He was alone, his own light, in his own dark world.

The Magician's Theft

He startled awake from another dream and automatically reached for the pen on the night stand. He moved too fast and knocked the pen and dream journal to the floor. Cursing, he winced as he shot a glance at the alarm clock.

3:01.

He groaned, fell back onto his pillow, and lay there trying to focus on the dream remnants. Something to do with a brightness, a swirling. Something to do with losing something.

CRAAACK. BOOM. A storm. Big one.

The man pushed himself up and headed for the nearest window. Naturally, he stumbled over the pen and journal. Bending to pick them up, his back objected about mid-bend so he just continued his stagger to the window and pulled back the liner curtain.

"My god."

The sky throbbed in a barrage of quick-cut lightning. So much lightning slashed through the air that the night shone pure white. Yet, the individual bolts scratched black against the sky in a bizarre, shattering mosaic of negative light, a nightmare of psychotic physics.

Something had to be up with her.

He looked around for the remote. The screen snapped to life. Black symbol lightning bolts splattered across the screen. They stuck like bent daggers in a wash of digital red rain that must have covered 20 counties or more.

Something bad about this one. He had to get to the tower.

He had been dreaming of tornadoes for several weeks. Most of them appeared as distant black-ribbed mouths, perfect funnels limberly tearing through bucolic, quilted landscapes of fenced fields, white mid-Western farm houses, and emerald forests. They always left a trail of vaporized dream-images clouding perfectly blue skies. Fields, houses, forests. Pfft, pfft, pfft.

He usually watched the riverine courses of destruction from a very safe distance, some high, bare mountain top. He could see the far-off explosions, imagine the noise and confusion, the sheer terror of those caught in their path, but he heard nothing, absolutely nothing. He tracked them like an astronomer eyes meteors and comets, or a naturalist the movements of predatory beasts.

Eyeing them from such a distance did not ease his discomfort, however. He always seemed to be alone and his options for escape minimal—where do you go from a mountain top? And no matter how far away he was, he knew they were watching him as closely as he watched them. And when one suddenly stopped…and turned…as if to look right at him…that's when he usually woke up.

He believed tornadoes possessed a cunning intelligence, mercurial and perverse. Like a vicious feline assassin, he had written in his journal that they stalked their victims with a professional disinterest and an unrelenting determination to claim whatever payment their unseen master is owed.

A tornado wants what it wants and nothing else suffices, he wrote.

It will leave a baby in a tree, safe, unscathed, a half a mile from where she was ripped from her father's arms. The father is left impaled on a utility pole, a broom handle rammed through his heart in a surgical precision unmatched by human skill.

The Arabs believed tornadoes were demons—djinns, dark messengers of the gods—who screamed out of the western deserts, the land of the dead, on missions of repossession. They fed on the righteous as well as the sinner. Their victims were the gods' victims and since no one knew how the gods cast lots, no amount of praying could guarantee safety.

Fear of the djinns was the source of the ancient injunction against giving a stranger your name. A stranger could be a djinn in disguise sent by a jealous god to steal your soul, to reclaim what had been lent. They were feared, but they were also holy, for sometimes it was Jehovah who spoke out of the whirlwind. Regardless, they were the executors of an unknown judgment against which no one could appeal.

We all both dread and invite such judgment. Perhaps it's the idea that we have been gifted with something beyond our means—with a special kind of life, a consciousness, a knowledge somehow incomplete and therefore perhaps stolen, not quite ours to keep. If it were ours, would we not have it whole and forever?

Of course, we hope not to be snatched away and, sometimes, may even act surprised when we are. But somehow we know that whatever happens, no matter our cries of expediency, we get what we deserve. We are, somewhere deep down, the guilty thieves that we perceive ourselves to be.

Mutable, transcendent intelligence giving us what we think we deserve—that's why tornadoes terrify us, why they fascinate us.

We seem to come closest to experiencing the unspeakable power of the divine through our contact with inexplicable and terrifying destruction. In fully experiencing the relentless power and intelligence of a messenger of death we know to our very core that there is something miraculous operating in the universe, something beyond the dry numbers-game of science. And in that undeniable knowledge there lies hope for even the vilest of thieves. Violent, mutable, and intelligent. If a tornado can change course so can we.

Thieves to kings. Kings to gods.

Sometimes in his dreams a twister would land beside him, a Jacob's ladder fallen from a wordless heaven. He strained to understand its silent spinning, see a way into and through its impenetrable, inhuman walls, find a foothold to climb up and ask what its demon name might be, what it wanted of him, of the human race. He encountered them so often over the years that his respect for them was great, but somehow over the past few weeks he had come to feel less fear when they approached.

For some perverse or brave or insane reason he was compelled to extend his hand to them—literally extend his hand, his open, turned up palm to a tornado spinning in a black fury right in front of him.

Twice, one obliged him and hopped onto his palm. It spun there, soft, cool, amazingly light. He even juggled it from palm to palm like a clown with a broom handle act. It was alive; he unmistakably sensed that it enjoyed the playing. Whatever its motivation, it clearly engaged him. It also wanted to tell him something. He could feel an energy directed toward him, a primitive urgency, a moaning, but it was so alien. He was so alien. How could such a gap be bridged?

When he played with the second one there was no deaf-mute attempt at verbalizing. Instead, he was absorbed into its skin, or rather it enveloped him at once like an amoeba surrounding a mote of food. He momentarily entered a clear, liquid void, calm—enchanting, but ultimately the nature of its quality, its qualities, he couldn't grasp. There wasn't time or time wasn't an issue.

He was almost immediately thrown into another dream. He had been invited into a very special place, but in his clumsiness, he had boorishly squandered the opportunity. He had violated a holy place. He had been brave and clever, but also arrogant and naive. His indiscretion had been answered with nothing but a quick trip through an inverted black hole.

Still, he felt lucky. Such sacred transgressions often end in death or madness. As far as he knew, he was in neither realm. But that's a judgment call.

Two days later, in another dream, he watched from the sidewalk of a crowded, narrow city street, a white vortex touch down beside an idling yellow cab. It came down so fast and with such intelligent authority that he was utterly petrified. The tornado extended into the twilight sky and seemed to be infinite black space itself, transformed and poured down into a single, intensely bright point of white, whirling light.

In a swirling instant of inter-dimensional transformation the maelstrom turned into a dark-haired, elegantly dressed woman—regal, haughty. Perhaps even a little frightened behind her cold, reserved expression.

She was already walking when she flashed from tornado to her human form. She stared straight ahead, unblinking, completely oblivious to him and the several gawking pedestrians gathered on the other side of the street.

The cab door on the street side opened without a word from her and she slipped onto the back seat. Impulsively, he jumped in the cab with her. There was so much he wanted to ask her. He had been unable to talk to the playful, black-hole wind, but a beautiful woman? He could talk to a beautiful woman.

Inside the cab she continued to stare straight ahead. The cab didn't move. He gazed into her powder white face, dumb struck with the closeness of her unearthly beauty.

Such beauty.

He was filled with light and emptied of all heaviness. His being was totally enthralled. Love, ecstasy, absolute joy—ethereal transcendence. He was floating. Floating. On the moon. Floating—lost in the infinite magnitude of his heart's utter bliss.

And all in a glance.

Alone with a tornado enfleshed, a goddess fallen from heaven, an archetype in a city cab.

He was alone…with god…in a cab…and she slowly turned her face to look into his. A faint smile crossed her lips and she waited. She waited for him to say something.

He had no idea what to say.

He couldn't hold the tension…sublime…ridiculous.

He woke up.

He initially wanted to cry, wanted to curl into a small, small ball and die. But there was something about her and the woman in the tower, something that connected the three of them.

He knew he was getting close to something extraordinary, something wonderfully and utterly transformative. He hadn't seen his veiled storyteller in a while. It was time.

He looked through the curtains again. The sky glowed green. Tornado green. Stay-in-the-house-in-the-closet green. But he couldn't stay safe and dry. He had to go to her.

As he pulled on his trousers, he checked the television again, scanning the stations for news of washed out bridges, specific flooded creeks. He'd have to take the long way if….

CRAAACK, BOOOM.

"God!"

The strike was so close he hunched his back and raised his fists in a defensive posture. Fizzle, pop. The television screen went black. Smell of ozone.

CRACK, BOOM roar of a train. Demon train. No tracks around there. None for miles.

A tornado.

CRAAACK, BOOOOM.

He fell to his knees and crawled quickly to the closet. Throw shoes out, go fetal, pray.

"Damn, the mattress."

CRACK, BOOM roar of a train passing. Passing close.

He opened the closet door, stood and ran to the bed. He yanked the mattress off the bedsprings and dragged it into the closet on top of him.

Pounding rain, lashing winds.

But the train was passing away.

Passing close, close…but away. Heading…where? Listen. Heading for her.

He pushed the mattress off. He jerked his field jacket from its hanger, slipped on the first shoes he could find and, pulling the mattress behind him, headed for the Jeep.

The ground was soaked. A peat bog. He threw the mattress in the back and crawled in behind it. He hopped over the seats to the steering wheel. Ignition. Lights. Deep breath. He slammed into reverse, spun the Jeep around, and headed toward the tower.

He held to the steering wheel like it was the last ticket out of hell. His fiery concentration burned the rising waters back and apart. Lightning fell right and left, but it never dared strike before him. His fearlessness was no bluff. He didn't flinch as strike after strike sounded beside him as if they were announcing the on-calls waiting at St. Peter's gate.

For awhile the universe actually retreated before his prophet-fired temperament.

Luckily, no bridges were out. As fired up as he was, downed bridges would not have stopped him. He would have driven right into the waters and joined that limbo crowd at heaven's door. In floods, just a few inches of raging water can tumble a car down stream as if it were no more than an empty beer can.

Deception works so well on the fearful and arrogant.

He jockeyed his way through the downed trees and snapped power lines of the suburbs and pulled onto the road leading to the tower. Out in the country the rain only increased its already steel-pounding intensity. He could barely see a thing in the silver solidity of its fierce, blinding display, but he knew the road well enough. He even dreamed about that road. So he pressed on with the will of his deep desire, not the reasonableness of instinct.

And then he rounded a short curve and rammed into a downed oak.

His head slammed into the windshield just about the time the air bag released. He lost consciousness. When he blinked awake, in what seemed but mere moments, his head rested on the back of the seat and he was staring at the truck's blue covered ceiling. The rain and lightning seemed to be at nearly the same intensity as it had been when he hit the brakes. Of course, that was not a good measure of time passage. His radio clock flashed 12:00 as it had since he bought the Jeep.

However, he could feel the goose egg rising on his forehead. He dabbed at the blood tracking down and across his wrinkled brow. It was plentiful. He swiped at the wound with his jacket sleeve, stared at the dark tattoo it made on the green cotton. Plentiful blood.

He opened the door and stepped out into the rain.

Liquid needles. The rain was bitterly cold. Still, he leaned back against the Jeep and faced straight up into the dazzling night. The rain felt great on his wound. But he knew it wouldn't feel good on his chest, yet there was no choice. He needed a bandage.

Off came the field jacket and then the t-shirt. A twist around the fists and a swift pull. He wrapped the halved piece around his forehead, slipped quickly back into the jacket, and stood there blankly staring at the ground.

Loud hissing drew his attention to the front of the Jeep. He smiled: cracked cartoon headlights revealing swirls of steam rising into the air like indifferent ghosts.

This Jeep was going nowhere.

He could see the tower far to his right. It glowed silver. His spirits revived. The mattress would be a problem, even if he did manage to get it there. Maybe she had some plastic sheeting. Right. He'd never seen anything in or around her place that dated past 1880. She'd have blankets, though. Nice, dry blankets.

A loud crack of thunder brought him back to his more pressing needs. Another crack immediately followed. And another. The sky was green fire. And then he heard the train. He started running toward the tower. Straight down the hill, into the rocks. Water seeking its home. Foot seeking a stub. He tumbled into a creek bed and started rolling in the rushing waters. And then something yanked him out of the water and set him on a rock ledge.

"Señor. Señor?"

An old man in a black plastic poncho was standing over him offering a hand.

"Sí," he said. "It is okay. The mistress sent me. There is a small cave not far from here. Come with me."

"Who the hell are you? Where did you come from? Did you just grab me out of the water like…like that?"

"The mistress sent me. Hurry. The storm is upon us."

Again he felt strong hands pull him up and set him standing.

"It is okay. Vámanos."

He nodded in stunned agreement and was pulled forward in the wake of the old man's commanding presence. A quick few yards down the creek they came to an overhang of limestone. The man stopped and motioned him to duck and go under. He hesitated for just a second, but a crack of thunder and the man's urgent call to "vete, vete" hurried him in. He stooped along for a few more yards in the dark only scraping his head a couple of times. It became so dark he had to feel his way along the walls with his hands. He felt a sudden shock of electricity and light poured into the cave from behind. He turned. The man was carrying a torch.

"We keep it here, in case," the man said flatly. "Go on. There is a crawl space then a ladder. The cave is very safe. There are two ways out if the flood waters ever get too high. Don't worry. The mistress knows where this place is."

He shrugged. At least he could see. He crouched on a few more steps before he had to get on his hands and knees. He looked back once and saw the torch lit face of the old man, expressionless, nodding him on. A few more yards and he was on his belly and the light was less bright. He had been out of the rain for a couple of minutes and the noise of the storm grew distant and then it was completely gone. In the silence he began to question what he was doing there. He was getting a little scared. Who was this guy? How would she have known he was coming? This was spooky. Very spooky. He slowed and was about to stop when he bumped into the ladder. He climbed up counting the steps. Seven. There was another narrow passage at the top and he had to crawl a little more. But there was a faint light in front of him so he didn't feel so claustrophobic.

The tunnel narrowed and he pushed through with his shoulders tightly squeezed against the slick surface of the walls. He came out into a large round space. Two torches were already lit. A small campfire burned briskly, encircled with melon-sized white stones. The smoke swirled up and through a hole in the cave ceiling directly overhead.

"It's like a kiva," he said aloud, his fear evaporating as he scooted his way to the other side of the fire and folded his legs, strangely relaxed.

"Yes, it is," the man replied. "I came here earlier to prepare it. You never know what a storm might bring. Here, take off that wrap and put this on."

The old man handed him a scarf with a dark green poultice set in the center of its folds.

"Just wrap it around your head," he commanded.

"Do what?"

"The mistress says she tells you things but that you don't hear her."

"I hear her," he scowled as he clumsily took off the T-shirt wrap and bowed his head into the scarf.

"I mean, you can't understand her or you don't know how to apply what she shares, the pictures she places in your mind."

"She is not like me. We think differently," he said, his tone a little lighter as he tied off the bandage and felt its warmth take immediate effect. The old man was nonplussed by his defensiveness and acted neither humble nor aloof. He was simply direct.

"But you like her, do you not?" the old man continued. "You want to hear what she has to say?"

"Yes. Yes, I do. On both counts. I just feel less assured around her for some reason. I mean I…." His voiced trailed off.

"She is very powerful," the man declared. "Anyone would feel her power and be cautious."

"I don't know if it's caution," he hedged.

"There is no shame in caution. I have a story. Would you mind if I told you a story?"

"No," he grinned. "I…uh…like stories." He felt inexplicably like a shy guest, a lost relative suddenly reunited with a family he didn't know he had. A family that appeared out of nowhere and saved his life. Stories would be fine. Just fine.

"The mistress says I should tell you a story. She says you feel most at home when you hear stories. I asked her where you were from that you didn't feel at home. She just laughed. We've known each other a long time. Anyway, I think I know how you feel. I like to hear the old stories. It seems to fill something inside, something here."

He touched his heart with the tips of his fingers.

"Not that I am empty. It is like a hand reaching out. That is what the stories are. A gentle hand that connects us to each other. It deepens our connection with…with the stars? The whole sky? And with the earth. Those places inside us that need touching. That is where the stories go.

"The stories tell me something that is like what I have always known. When I hear them it is like I knew them already, but better, deeper, like they are really mine. It is like I will carry them with me when I leave. And then I become the story? The carrier for the story? Yes?"

He nodded in mute agreement with the old man.

"I think that is what the mistress means. You have lost that sense of belonging…here."

The old man pointed forcefully to the ground, his fingers closed together like he was dropping seeds.

Then very gently the old man touched his own heart again, "And here."

His heart flushed hot with the old man's truth, burned in its own sudden emptiness.

"But I know it happens," the old man continued. "I know how it is lost. I have seen the young men, how they swagger and yet hide, how they will not water the seeds of their heart, not let the stories grow inside them."

The old man gazed down at the fire. They were silent for several minutes. Any residual fear of the man had disappeared, gone in the pale white smoke and through the hole in the cave up into the cleansing heavens.

"Let the winds take it," he whispered. He must have said it out loud though he didn't intend to. When he looked up the old man was looking at him in a way that was both comforting and strangely distant.

"This is a story best heard inside," the old man whispered and again touched his chest. "Close your eyes. You will see it better."

Smiling like a sad child, he did as he was told.

"So," the old man said, "let the wind carry our voices to the young men's hearts." He brought his hands together at his heart, bowed to the fire and closed his eyes.

***

In the old days, before time was kept in a box on a wall there was a man who loved his child very much. Now all men who are men love their children. This is so and should always be. And men who are men love their children more than life itself. For love gives meaning to a man's life and nothing else will do. But this man, this man was crazy in love with his child. He loved his child as if she were his life. And there is a difference, as you shall see.

The child's mother had died in childbirth and the man did not want his child to die, did not want her to go through what her mother had suffered. The man wanted to keep the child the same. He wanted nothing to change. He wanted time to stop. His love was wrapped in fear.

Every day this man dressed his child in a white ruffled dress with ribbons and bows. He tied fresh flowers at her shoulders and in her hair and across her chest and back. Each morning and every night he brushed her hair, washed her soft rosy cheeks, and sang to her songs of praise. Never did she hear a single word of discouragement or rebuke. A goddess in a shrine received no less devotion than she did.

The girl was very beautiful. And very happy. At least that is what the man believed.

The girl was allowed outside only when he accompanied her. Even then she could only go to a particular park close to their home. The park was at the edge of a large forest of white birch with clear paths and a stone wall ten feet high that encircled it and marked the furthest she could wander. But this presented no problems for her because she knew of no other worlds.

Her father liked to sit at a spot beside a small grove of trees in the very center of the park. He brought a high swivel chair so that no matter where the girl went he could track her as she gathered flowers and leaves and sometimes, after a rainstorm, fallen nests. At first he would not let her go near the wall, but gradually, over months, she got closer and closer until he no longer noticed.

Soon, her favorite spot became a small niche in the wall where she had seen lizards hide. She began poking at the niche with a birch switch and little by little the wall gave way until one day there was a hole large enough and deep enough for her to peek through to the other side.

Beyond the wall she saw a bright river whose waters rippled over large smooth stones left from an abandoned bridge. Large, beautiful salmon splashed about as if trying to gulp down the sun. And beyond the bridge grazing in a meadow of red flowers was a white unicorn.

The girl's heart raced as she gazed into this bright new world. She opened her mouth to call to her father but inside her head she heard a soft music and saw the face of the unicorn looking deep into her eyes asking her to keep his world a secret. There was a power in the music and in the unicorn that she could not disobey. Something in her wanted it to be a secret, too. Looking through the hole at the beautiful river, the fish, the stones, and graceful beasts made her feel powerful and special. So, she agreed not to tell her father about the hole or the river or the unicorn.

But secrets are hard to keep, and slowly, she felt less and less powerful and more and more lonely as she looked into a world she could not touch and could not speak of. Finally, she refused to go into the park at all. She refused her father's questions then refused to come out of her room. Soon, she refused to let him brush her hair or sing his songs. The father indulged his daughter at first for he only wanted to please her, but as days turned into weeks and weeks into months he became worried. And when, during a raging summer storm, she abruptly left their evening meal saying she was ill, the fear that wrapped his love began to choke him and he became furious. As if possessed, he followed her up the stairs and pulled her from her bed. He held her tightly by the shoulders and shook her and shook her, demanding that she tell him what was wrong.

"The wall!' she cried. 'The wall!"

And then she collapsed. The man went pale with terror. Panicked, he picked her up and carried her out into the punishing rains and into the park. The sky was full of lightning and winds howled through the trees. There was a tremendous crack of thunder and the man looked up and jumped away just as a tree came crashing down onto the wall, knocking a wide section of it to the ground. In that instant the girl's eyes opened and she hugged her father and kissed him and thanked him and thanked him. He brought her back to their home and placed her in bed. She was already asleep.

The next day the girl was up at dawn and asking to go the park.

She let her father brush her hair and sing his songs and dress her in her white ruffled dress covered in flowers. When he asked her if she loved him she looked deep into his eyes. He held her gaze for a moment but then looked away. She laughed and took his hand and pulled him to the door.

"Come on, come on. Let's run." Together they ran out the door.

There had been little damage to the park. Only the single tree had fallen. When the girl asked to climb to the other side of the wall, her father could not refuse her. He lifted her through the breach and then he climbed across the tree and onto the wide river bank. There were small trees and berry bushes along the bank and across the river there was a flower strewn meadow. The fish still splashed in the waters, but no animals grazed among the flowers.

The girl said nothing about the missing unicorn and was content to pick berries, chase lizards, and dance at the edge of the water. When she knelt by the river the salmon came up to her and allowed her to stroke their smooth, glistening bodies. The man's worries vanished. Everything seemed to be as it was before the storm. Only now, instead of his chair, he brought bread crumbs so the girl could feed the fish.

It was a delightful time for the father and child but after a week or so the little girl asked if they might cross the river. The father had never refused her, and he would not now.

"That's fine, but why don't we wait," he suggested, "wait until we can build a new bridge? You could throw stones in the river on top of the old bridge. When there are enough stones we will be able to cross and not be caught in the rapids. Every day we can bring a sack of rocks, special white rocks that I will gather for just this purpose. We want it to be a strong bridge and a beautiful one, and that's what we will have. Soon, we will be able to cross. We can start tomorrow."

The girl readily agreed.

The next day the girl and father went to the river and as he promised he brought a sack full of beautiful, egg-shaped white stones. He found a small tree to sit under and he watched as she threw all the stones in the water.

"See?" he said. "A great start. You've done your work, now play."

She laughed in delight and resumed her berry picking, lizard chasing, and feeding of her wild fish. Her father was very happy.

Day after day they went to the river. The girl was a little puzzled as to why the bridge appeared not to rise, but her father assured her it was rising, and that bridges were hard to build and that her work would be rewarded. She loved her father so she believed him, but within a month she began to have nightmares.

Late one night she woke and called for her father. There was no answer. She called again but he did not come. She left her bed and noticed that the front door was open. A distant figure walked toward the park. Silently, she followed.

When she got to the breach in the wall she stopped and tip-toed a few steps to the left. The hole she made from the lizard's niche had not been damaged by the falling tree. She looked through it and watched as her father waded into the waters and began filling a sack with the stones she had thrown.

Her heart broke.

She cried as she watched him gather the last stone and turn to walk back through the breach. Just past the wall, he stopped and looked back at the river.

"I'm sorry," he whispered, "but she is all I have."

Then he turned and hurried back toward their home.

The girl wanted to run to him and tell him he was wrong, that he had more than her (than the her he thought she was), that he had stolen what could be by clinging to what was. And though she could not wipe away her tears, neither could she turn back. After he passed, she walked through the breach and into the river. She stood in the cold, rushing waters and looked across to the meadow.

"Please," she sobbed. "Please let me cross."

She reached down, pulled up a rock from the old bridge and flung it into the waters. She reached in again and again. With each throw, a light pierced from the water into the night, and the bridge grew higher, and the salmon in the river gathered around her and in their mouths were more stones. Soon there was a golden, flowing light that arched over the river and danced into the meadow.

Then another light, bright and silver, streamed out of the forest and began swirling around and around, creating a round door of light and music, a gentle whirlwind of strange beauty at the end of the enchanted bridge.

From the center of the vortex stepped the beautiful, white unicorn. It looked like a horse made of pure light. A strong beam of golden stardust burst from its forehead. The girl looked back at the wall and whispered, 'Good-bye.' She stepped onto the bridge of light and crossed over to the other side.

The unicorn waited for her. She stroked its fine white muzzle and climbed onto its back. The unicorn leaped once and disappeared into the vortex, which immediately evaporated leaving only a sparkling of silver dew on the cold ground while the meadow returned to utter silence.

The dawn filled with the frightened calls of birds as the father's relentless screams rang back and forth between his home and the edge of the river. As he ran, he called out for his daughter over and over, called until his voice was a raw rasp whispering the girl's name into the mute day.

Finally, his legs could bear his weight no more and he fell to his hands and knees at the edge of the river. He stared into his reflection, grown red and yellow in the light of the morning sun. A salmon swam by in the waters beneath his face. And then he saw her in the rippling mirror of the river. He saw her step onto the bridge of light, saw a man holding an egg-shaped stone, a swirling liquid doorway.

A magician. A thief. The father looked up from the waters and gazed into the dark forest beyond the meadow. He rose and stepped unto the white bridge stones. They slipped beneath him and he fell into the water. He stood again, and again the stones gave way. The man cursed and slapped the water with his fists and the water turned black and cold, deeper, and more swift. The man plunged head first into the river, yet the waters and the stones threw him back to the bank, shaking him off like a dog shaking water from its back. The man could not cross.

In the days and months that followed, the man frantically tried to build a bridge across the river but no matter what he tried, the river destroyed his work in the night.

A year passed, and another and another. Day after day he walked alone to the foot of the abandoned bridge. But one day he saw a salmon floating dead in the river and he lost all hope. He screamed out the girl's name and fell to his knees and wept. A single tear fell into the river and a salmon swam up to the man.

It was a large, silvery fish unlike any he had ever seen. He reached out to touch it. The fish did not swim immediately away, but let him stroke its smooth skin for a few moments before it leapt up and turned to swim to the other side of the river. In its sparkling wake the white stones of the bridge rose up.

The man stood and stared at the stones, not believing what he saw. The salmon leapt again and the man gingerly stepped onto the stones. They did not give way as they had before but seemed to rise to meet his stride. He took another step and another. At the end of the bridge the salmon leapt once more and vanished underneath the river bank. The man continued walking, his heart pounding as each footfall brought him closer to the other side. He stopped at the end of the bridge. He closed his eyes, held his breath, and jumped.

The light changed. The meadow and the forest beyond were bathed in bright moonlight. He looked behind him and the river was a distant ribbon of gold, miles away and far, far below him. A splash sounded deeper into the forest. The father followed the sound into the pearl-gray darkness.

Deep in the woods, standing on a rocky ledge with his crooked back against a majestic oak, a wizard peered into a small pool. He sang a soft lullaby as he raised a fishing pole and dropped his line lazily into the still water.

The father crouched down and scurried behind the nearest tree. The wizard swayed slightly to his left and glanced to where the man hid.

He sang a little louder, "What is that slippery, silvery fish flashing through the streams of my soul, my soul? Who is the one who won't be caught no matter the lengths I go?"

The man stepped out from behind the tree and stood in defiance of the wizard's taunt. The wizard lifted his line, saw nothing on the hook, and lowered it back down.

"Who are you?" the father hissed. "Tell me your name."

"You know," the wizard said, lifting his head as if addressing the stars, completely ignoring the father, "truth is, she never is caught, but only voluntarily surrenders when the light shines just so, and even then, the fisher, finally wise, releases her back into the mirrored pool and pretends he never did so."

The wizard looked directly at the father who stood all at once beside him.

"You're too late," the wizard whispered and vanished like a mist into the pool.

The father looked into the waters. He saw in a reflection the wizard floating upside down above him, twisted as if he were a hook and the man the fish.

"She left me," the wizard smiled. "I tried to do for her the best I could. Gave her everything I thought she wanted. Kept her so pure, like a goddess. But there's only one place for goddesses to go, so she left me. Left me. Stolen by angels. I try to catch her. I know she's there somewhere in the depths of the sullen waters, the vastness of heaven's hair, but what would I do with her once I caught her? What have you done, sentimental old fool?"

The man spun around and swung at the wizard with his fists. He swung at air. The wizard floated on his side above the pool. It swirled black and electric blue, a furious maelstrom.

"There are many terrors in life, sir," the wizard yawned above the tempest, "but none so sad as fear of growing old. None so sad as a man who fears for himself more than he loves his child. Even onto death. You want to know my name? Tell me who you are."

The wizard took a deep breath and held it, freezing the father's attention momentarily. And then the wizard burst out laughing and suddenly spun like a dervish on fire, transforming into a flaming red salmon flapping about in the crackling air and gasping for breath like a demonic clown. The man, crazy for revenge, jumped at the fish which evaporated between his fingers like a mist and he fell screaming into the maelstrom, down, down, down, forever screaming his daughter's name, forever swimming after the magician's theft, swimming into the darkness of his endless sorrow, forever swimming and swimming until for him there was no more swimming to be done.

***

The storyteller grew silent. He took three deep breaths and said, "Thus it was told in the days before time." The old man then threw a handful of sand into the fire, sending colored sparks crackling into the air. Still entranced but puzzled, his listener thought for a moment and then was horrified at the old man's tale.

"He killed the girl, his daughter?" he asked, his voice not hiding his contempt. "Symbolically? Is that what you're saying?"

"You are not happy with this version? The mistress said it might be so. There are many versions and we've time enough. Listen."

Taking a deep breath again the old man closed his eyes. His captive listener stared at him, his brow deeply furrowed. The old man's eyes opened and he gestured for his audience to close his. With a sigh and more than a touch of uneasiness, he was obeyed.

***

The man swam and swam and swam, the old man calmly offered, following the magician throughout the underworld looking for his daughter. But the magician always led him away from her, let her grow and learn and live the full life of a human being.

The daughter watched her father's travels from the surface of a magic pool in the garden of the high castle where she lived with her husband, the Unicorn King. Compassion for him grew in her heart as the years passed and he grew old and bent. The wizard taunted and taunted him, but the father was relentless in his pursuit. Finally, the daughter's hatred melted and she asked the magician to lift the curse.

The magician led the father into a narrow tunnel that slowly spiraled up and up and finally emptied at the entrance to the cavernous throne room of a magnificent castle. The father crawled out of the water of the tunnel and breathed air for the first time since he had fallen into the maelstrom. He stood in the enormous room, a completely black man in tattered, dripping rags, tiny and bent and as thin as the thinnest of urchins. He was a black crow cipher, a burnt husk seed, a fading mote under the dome of heaven.

Trembling, he held the back of his neck against the pain as he looked up to the heights of the expansive room. Lights from hundreds of toweringly tall stained-glass windows crisscrossed the giant oaken arches in a dizzying array of colors. Doves fluttered from sill to sill, but they were so high that not a whisper was heard. The ceiling was pure gold and clusters of diamonds formed constellations, the moon, and the sun.

His gaze traced down the massive stone walls blackened with the smoke of countless days and untold lives. His eyes rested on the throne. It was narrow, carved of black marble, and draped with heavy, blood red brocade. He counted seventeen steps leading to its seat. Its back was as high as three men.

Save the distant doves, the room was empty and it seemed it had been so for years.

The man stood there quietly and remembered his daughter.

"You were all I had," he whispered. "You were all I had."

He looked up at the ceiling once more and turned to walk back into the waters of his grief, but then he heard a voice—no more than a drop of dew on a leaf, but it was there—he heard a small voice, a small voice crying from behind the throne.

"Turn around. Turn around, Grandfather. The room will grow to fill your needs. This place is your heart, Grandfather. Turn around."

And the old man turned and his rags fell from him like so much dust and he was clothed in sable and velvet and upon his head was a golden crown. Before him on the throne was a boy, his boy, his grandson. And next to the boy was the daughter, his beautiful daughter and in her arms a babe, radiant and more lovely than the stars.

He rushed to his daughter and fell to his knees, pressing his weary face into her belly and sobbing so as to shake the earth. She handed the babe to her husband and leaned down and embraced her father's face with her hands. She looked deeply into his eyes and said, "I love you."

The old man could only mouth the words back through his trembling, tear-stained lips. His daughter, the queen, helped him to rise and turned to introduce him to her husband, the Unicorn King, the Magician who had stolen the girl and led the man to this glorious place. He bowed deeply before the old man and slowly, gently held out the babe for the old man to hold.

***

The storyteller took three deep breaths and said again, "Thus it was told in the days before time." He threw another handful of sand into the fire. The young man opened his eyes and pressed the scarf at his wound. The swelling was down. He didn't know what to think.

"And you approve of this version? I can hear it in your voice," he said.

"What you hear is what you hear," the old man answered flatly. "Young men want approval. They want the world to be a nipple, giving them whatever they ask. And they wonder why women are so sad. They wonder why their own hearts grow cold and hard even as they long to be warm and eternally young.

"Approval. Perhaps that ending will ring true when you do not have to have it so. Saying it does not make it so. That is why we pray our stories are taken to the young men's hearts, not to their heads. In a heart that is open, all endings are true and generous. I hold no animosity either way. Perhaps, tomorrow you will see with different eyes, the eyes of your heart. And if so, all's the better."

He looked up toward the hole in the cave's ceiling. The darkness was lessening, the rain had all but stopped. He stood in a single fluid movement.

"The storm is almost over," the old man said in his dry, emotionless tone. "I must get back to the mistress."

"Uh, wait. I'll go with you," the young man stammered, not quite knowing what else to say.

"No, I don't think the mistress wants you just yet."

"Is that what she said?"

"No. But if she wanted you, we'd be there by now."

"What are you talking about?"

"You are still unhappy with the ending, are you not? Bueno. I have a few more minutes. I will speak directly, clearly to what you need to know. Keep your eyes open. Listen. Be ready.

"Terror can rescue those who've forgotten beauty, those who have been so pummeled with ill luck that they've numbed themselves to all feelings, but especially beauty and love. Beauty and love brought nakedly before these tender souls would be too cruel a punishment. It would remind them of what they believe they can never have, what they have never deserved, have been deprived of because of a sin they feel they have committed in their heart, a sin greater than any human law they may have violated. It is a bloody knife, a unicorn's horn ripped from the beast's lifeless body, that gouges a pit in their heart so deep all reflections of decency are swallowed whole and turned to coldest hatred."

"For a few, nothing can pull them from this abyss of self-loathing. They are no longer human. They have become evil djinns, messengers of soul-death.

"Beyond the call of human redemption, they become servants of terror itself, answering unconsciously to forces beyond their comprehension.

"Terror can be grace reanimating a soul with a sense of wonder and the realization that it is beauty, more than terror, that displays the divinity within the world. Why? Because it shows us that we matter. We matter. It shows that we are accomplices in the creation of the world. A great and terrifying responsibility.

"The unicorn, the tornado, call us to a new life, a renewed life. They catch us up in their terror, their beauty, and our dreams of petty control, our cleverness—all sucked into a relentless, unforgiving void. And yet, we can wake in the lap of love centered and ready to engage in the mystery again.

"To confront your fear is but the first step. Then you must find the queen, serve her, and through her find the kingdom of your heart. Service is for life. Life is for service. It is not a bondage. It is a joyous commitment, a communion. Only to those flung to the outer edges by their fear, their anger, their self-righteousness—only they feel bondage through their refusal to change, their refusal to enter into the swirl of life.

"Tornadoes, unicorns—they are fingers of divine creators enticing us into the swirling, mysterious darkness of existence so we might see a light unsurpassing in its beauty and in its infinite capacity to astound.

"Tornadoes are alive, mi amigo. And I am a tornado, a tornado sent by the mistress to tell you these things. Why she doesn't take you, I do not know. That is not my business. I only serve her. And that is the end of the story and now it is time for me to go."

The young man stared at him, puffed out an uncomfortable little laugh.

"I…I…. You're a…what?"

The old man's feet vanished in a black, swirling dust, a dust that swept up his body instantaneously. His face stretched wide in his first and last smile and he said, "You just do not listen." And then the old man's eyes disintegrated into a full blown, black-skinned tornado.

It just spun there, spun for an eternity, and then shot up through the hole in the cave and was gone. Gone, and the young man rose up, too, the blood drained from his face as if to be drawn into the heavens with the *thing*. His knees began to shake, then they buckled, sending him to his hands and knees, nauseous, head spinning.

He couldn't look up again for fear it would be there, returned to ask him his name, to take him to….

"Do not look up. Do not look up," he mumbled into the ground.

He stared at the wet cave floor for several breaths, then sat up and looked at his hands.

"This must be a dream," he declared loudly. "I'll look at my hands and I'll fly away."

He jumped up and banged his head against the slanted walls of the cave. He fell to the ground, rolled onto his back, eyes closed tightly. He was hyperventilating.

He was absolutely terrified.

He must have lain there for hours. At some point he fell asleep and when he woke he opened his eyes praying he would be in his own room. He wasn't. He was still on the cave floor. But the hole above him revealed blue sky. Unfortunately, it was too high for him to reach, so he had to crawl back down the tunnels. It took him half an hour, but he made it back to the entrance. There was very little water in the creek. The floodwaters had flashed through to the sea. He jumped over the narrow stream and trudged the few hundred yards to the tower.

The front door was open and she stood at the stove singing, stirring soup. He'd never even noticed the stove, had never seen her eat. She didn't turn when he walked in, but instantly began to talk exuberantly, like a school girl, like a woman in love.

"Don't you just adore violent weather? The first storm of the season. Heaven's music. The bride's processional. We're alive. Time to renew the spirit and soul of the world."

He just looked at her, amazed.

"You're cold, aren't you? And soaking? The soup is just about...yes. Ready. Cauliflower soup. My grandmother taught me. Old country recipe. Blankets are on the chair, there. Sit down. Here it is. Grandfather made these trays. Beautiful, aren't they? Four different woods."

She placed a bowl on the tray in front of him and then held out a tray of ice cubes.

"One ice cube," she admonished. "No more. Thick enough for just one cube and then just blow and it'll be fine. I have a story for you. I've written it. See?"

She pointed to a small red book lying on the armrest of his chair.

"Father loved to read and eat at the same time. He was impatient just like you. You read it while I sit on the porch and listen to the morning. Glad you're back, by the way. I missed you. Oh, and one thing—did you know a tornado was the inspiration for the shape of the tower? But you must've known that. Everyone knows a tornado is the spirit of a murdered woman tired of waiting for justice. Anyway, if you didn't, that will help you interpret the story."

He watched her go out onto the porch. It was the first time he'd ever seen her in daylight. Of course, she still wore the veil, but he could see a luminescence beneath it, some star-lit version of human skin, a softness. He didn't read the story that day. He grabbed the soup and joined her on the front porch. Together they listened to the morning.

The Blackberry Patch

The tornado haunted him for weeks.

Initially, he didn't tell the woman in the tower about it. At least nothing about the storyteller. She had been so happy that morning with her talk of soup and trays and ice cubes. He hadn't wanted to dampen her mood. Plus, the experience simply stunned him. That, and he didn't want her to think he was crazy. Of course, the first order of business was convincing himself that he wasn't crazy.

His intention had been to see her again within three days. Yet, a week passed and he had barely left his house. Merely looking at the car keys lying on the kitchen counter chilled his blood. Like an old defeated man, he found it easier to take to his bed.

When he had gone out into the storm he assumed there was a connection between her and the woman in his dreams, the one who he later determined had to be the storyteller's mistress. Once he reached the tower and saw her so open and vulnerable, so human, that notion of linkage evaporated. But once he left her charmed circle and returned to his home, doubts began to plague him. He prayed he was wrong. Still, there had to be some connection. Maybe not a linear one, but some dream algorithm, some functional, discernible aspect of the empirical world had to be working here, a solid, rational thing he could discover and grasp in his dullish, middle class mind. He had to get it straight, cut out all the extraneous information and get to the bare, simple physics of it all.

Like a good, by-the-books scientist, he went over the details time and time again. Over it and over it. All the permutations, all the if this, then this syllogisms. Over it and over it, but it came out the same every time.

Squirm as it might, it stuck to its circuitous route like a wyrm ouroboros, an idiot-dog monster chasing its coy mistress of a dead end tail.

What if they were the same woman? Confronted with this, would she kill him? Would the veil drop off and a blood-dripping skull open its maw and suck him screaming down into the pits of hell? Would she smile the loveliest of smiles just before she turned into a blackhole nightmare vortex and carried him off to a Prozac-zombied Oz? "Hi, my name's Pez. I'm from Sirius."

Seriously nuts.

He knew her, knew her well. How could you send someone you trusted, who trusted you, who held a special place in your heart, how could you send such a person to hell? She was not capable of being a demon.

Who was he kidding? Sure she was. Everybody was.

Hadn't the storyteller said that when the mistress wanted him she would simply take him? So it wasn't like the woman in the cab was a soul-sucking demoness all the time. She sent the old man to him as an emissary, a friend. It made more sense that he served the woman in the taxicab. She was a dream denizen, an inhabitant of another world. Clearly, the old man was of that ethereal, non-material persuasion.

That logic didn't help for long. What evidence did he have that the woman in the tower was real? He had no artifact from her.

So he went over it and over it.

And had he actually been ruminating over the reality of demons?

He finally convinced himself that none of that mattered. It was so much philosophy. Mind games. Cocktail chatter.

The scarf, however. The scarf with the ointment he had wrapped around his head at the old man's instruction. That mattered. That was real. In the scarf he had explicit, undeniable evidence that he had met… someone. He had his head wound and the scarf. Admittedly, the head wound could be explained by the wrecked car. The encounter with the old man and his story could be explained away by the fact that he had a head wound. Hallucination caused by trauma. But the scarf. Where did he get the scarf?

Maybe it had been lost by a couple on a picnic. They'd been caught in a sudden rain. Paper plates and half-empty Chinese take-out cartons tumbling about. Perhaps, the scarf had been unknotted for a kiss, flown away with laughter and napkins, wheeling about the meadow like hyper children. Or perhaps it had been lost from a passing convertible by a carefree, young lover standing in the wind to declare her love with a wild wave of a rainbow flag?

He might have just picked it up in his dazed, head-banged state. Made sense. Maybe.

But the ointment? The ointment was fresh. A scarf is blown away in a rain storm and flies for miles until it drifts down a hole in a cave over a fire and it is not only not soaking wet and not burned, but still has a fresh herbal ointment neatly packed into its folds?

Life may be strange. But not that strange.

He had met a man, a man who said he served a mistress, a man who was incredibly strong, wise, and fearless. He met a man who said he wasn't a man, but was a tornado. And then he actually did turn into a tornado. Dream stuff. Except he had the scarf. The damned scarf. What a miracle to have the scarf. And what a curse. The scarf was real, but he knew it wouldn't prove a thing no matter how well he told his story. You can hold a ray gun in your hand and swear a green man from Mars gave it to you, but if the transaction wasn't televised live, you had nothing. Nothing. A common scarf? Less than nothing.

There was only one person who would believe him. And he wasn't even sure if she was real. The longer he waited, though, the less sure he was that anything—anything—in his life was real. It came down to her.

Ten days he had waited, ruminated, worried. The Jeep was out of the shop. His head was only a little yellow around the stitches. Weather clear. New moon. 64 degrees. Wind out of the north at 10 to 15 miles an hour. Soul yellowing. Spirit black. Heart white. Head on fire. Sunset whenever you closed your eyes. Time to go.

The scarf lay beside him on the seat in a redwood jewelry box. He drove 35 miles per hour all the way and arrived maybe an hour before sunset. But the gate was down. He left the truck, put the box in his jacket pocket, and walked to the tower anyway. The front door was locked. She wouldn't be receiving visitors. This wasn't a relief. He didn't want a reprieve from this conversation. He wanted it over. He had to do something to kill time until sunset, something that wouldn't drive him to the point where he had to drive back home.

He headed toward the beach. The ocean's immensity, the relentless meeting of waves on rock, no matter how quiet or violent, always soothed his soul, washed away his smaller and greater fears, the detritus of any day, sometimes, it seemed, even of a lifetime.

He scooted through the last line of scrub oaks at the top of the dunes and started to run down the dune in a mad dash to the water. Then from the corner of his eye he saw her.

She was wading in the surf! He was so shocked he gasped and then stumbled, fell, and rolled all the way down to the flats. He sat up on his knees spitting out sand and wiping it from his face. He peeked out a squinted eye, hoping she hadn't seen him. But no such luck. She was laughing at him. Pointing and laughing.

"The boogie man after you?" she called, doubled over, her hand covering her mouth.

He scowled, but that only made her laugh harder.

"You are priceless," she choked out between laughs. "I'm sorry. I don't mean to make fun. We all have our problems. But you are so serious. Even when you go to the ocean. Such a serious man."

"I don't know what you're talking about," he said red-faced, not looking at her, but standing and brushing the sand off his shirt. "I have a sense of humor," he stuttered. "I don't know what you…. I…don't know. Geez, damn sand."

She had him completely flustered.

"It isn't that you lack a sense of humor. It is more what makes you laugh. You don't like not knowing, do you?" she said as she walked up, took him by the arm, and started strolling down the beach. "I read that thinking people view life as a comedy and feeling people see it as a tragedy. That's too easy, don't you think?"

"Well, I think, I feel that it's probably…"

"Don't answer, Jack. Can I call you Jack? Never mind. I'll just call you Jack and you can call me Jill. Just for today."

"Yeah, sure…Jill."

"Well, Jack, I've known many intelligent people who were the most tragically affected victims you'd ever not want to meet. Conversely, I've known sentimental fools who never met a stranger or an unhappy ending. So that's not really the issue, this thinking, feeling duality."

They walked on a little while in silence. She looked out at the ocean, pointed out some diving pelicans and a few sprays that might have been whales. He nodded silently, giving over his doubts into her capable arms and letting his consciousness roll on in blank serenity. About half a mile down the beach they came to an inlet of a small lagoon. The tide was in so they could go no further along the coast without getting wet or taking a very long detour.

"Shall we turn back?" he asked quietly, not really thinking they should. It was an automatic question. He was still very much entranced by her presence and the calming surge of the waves.

"You want to ask me something, don't you?"

"I don't know," he whispered.

"Again, that bothers you, doesn't it? Not knowing. What was it Socrates said? 'Knowledge begins with I don't know.' And the Zen masters? Zen mind, beginner's mind. Chop wood, carry water. I don't know is the beginning and the end. Here you are in the middle and you don't know. Come."

She pulled him over to a piece of driftwood lying at the base of a dune.

"Sit," she commanded. She sat beside him and clasped his hands in hers. "Desire and need," she said quietly, looking out into the darkening sea. "We think, or feel, whichever, that we need knowledge of everything, everything—or else we are pawns, fools, puppets. Ignorance, we are told, condemns us to a prison of unmet desires. If only we knew, then we would be complete. We would have power. Power like the gods. The tree of knowledge, the tree of immortality, would be ours, finally.

"Power. We are taught to believe we need power. That desire is the urge to power. Yes, you can feel it rising in you now—that hunger for power. I can feel it in your hands. Your eyes gaze out at that ocean and you want what it has. That is not what we want. You think you want the ocean. But what do you really want? Desire has come to mean the drive to possession. You had a fear of the ocean a while back. And now you desire it. The fear and the desire are one and the same. But look further than the either-or of possession."

"How do I do that?" he asked.

"How, indeed?" she laughed. "Shall we build a fire? The sun will be down soon. I'd like to sit out here for a while and watch the moon rise. Perhaps, tell you a story. It's time for one, don't you think?"

"Yes," he nodded. "A fire and a story would be nice."

He gathered some driftwood while she scooped out a pit in the sand with a flat stone. He thought about the old man, the last time he had a fire and a story. His doubts began to rise again. What if she was one of them? What if she were telling him just enough of the truth to lure him in? He had read somewhere that there isn't such a thing as pure evil. There's always just enough good in the person to allow them to deceive you. That was how cons worked, how bad politicians could rule a country for years before their venality was exposed.

There was so much he didn't know about her.

"Are you about done?" she called. "I've finished the pit and I have a small one going. It needs some bigger pieces."

She had a fire already? He reached into his pocket. He didn't have any matches, no lighter.

"Coming!" he yelled. He shook his head at the ridiculous suspicions. She was on the beach before he was. She had probably planned on a fire. He really didn't need to know how she started it.

She was sitting in profile facing the fire, the ocean in the background. The firelight penetrated her veil and he could see a faint silhouette of her face. He squinted and moved closer. She turned to face him and laughed. He tripped again. She scurried over to help him up.

"Jack, you sure take a lot of tumbles."

"Well, Jill, I'm glad you didn't name me Humpty Dumpty."

"Oh, I think they're pretty much the same. Here, let's pile these here and put these two on the fire. A good hour's worth."

"Nice fire," he said sitting beside her.

"I have my ways," she whispered, playfully leaning into him and clasping his hands again. "But now it's time for a story. You ready?"

"I don't know, but take it away, Jill."

"Good. Humor suits you. Now, look into the fire, into the wood where the fire eats hotly and watch as the embers become cities; cities of a magical place far, far away. See how each square, each cell of the wood turns to ash, becomes a home, a room, an individual life. Watch how even as it glows brightly in the center, the ash forms between the adjoining squares. Yet, still they glow, connected by the ash. Connected with desire. A desire that clothes them, allows them to burn even longer. Burn into forever. Love and longing need no gods for proof. Love and longing only need us."

***

Once upon a time there was a boy who lived in a blackberry patch. He didn't remember when he had not lived in a blackberry patch but he knew that one day he would leave it and make a difference in the world.

He lived with foxes and snakes; owls, ravens, and toads; otters and great bears. Each became as a brother to him. He learned their languages and did them small favors and so his name was known throughout the animal world. He warned young ones of danger. He told predators where they might find an old one who was ready to die. He mended wing and paw, warmed cold skin and cooled panting tongue. There was no animal that would refuse his request for help. They taught him the ways of the wild and of the unseen spirits who inhabited the seven realms.

One winter evening he woke from the dream realm and heard a distant voice call him. It was a voice he recognized but could not name, and he knew it was the call he had always longed to hear. So he packed everything he had, which was not much at all, into a bag fashioned of twigs and foxtails, and set out in the snow. He did not know how far he had to go or what dangers awaited him. He only knew he had to go, and each night he woke from a dream and there was a voice growing stronger, calling more desperately.

On and on he went following the dream voice deep into the snow covered forests at the top of the world. After many months he came to a blasted plain. Only a few scattered trees marked the far horizon. The sky was like a fire as he walked into the white, cold desert. But soon the sky turned black and though the moon came up and went down, the sun could not be seen. He traveled by starlight.

The voice called him on, and he followed as a bird follows the seasons. He followed for seven risings of the moon and he came to a castle broken and abandoned, the bones of dragons lying about, dead for a thousand years. Though frightened, he knew the source of the calling was inside that castle and he tightened his vine of a belt and went in.

Inside the castle keep he found a giant sound asleep, dead almost. The giant was covered in rags, though the boy could tell the rags were once those of a mighty king. He called out but the giant did not stir. Instead, the pink nose of a giant mouse peeked out from the mound of rags and wiggled.

"Hullo," said the boy. "I've come a long way to offer my services to the giant. Can you tell me what has happened here?"

"Who are you that I should tell you anything? Looks more like I should eat you," the mouse shot back.

"I'm the boy of the blackberry patch. I've saved many a cousin of yours from the talons of the silent owl. Please return the favor and tell me the giant's story, who he was and how he came to be in this sad state."

That was enough for the mouse who even in the darkest and coldest regions of the earth had heard of the kindness of the boy who lived in the blackberry patch. He lay down beside the boy and told him everything he knew about the giant.

"There was a witch who grew up with the giant. She loved him from the time they were small children. And he loved her, though he never told her. He was shy and one day would be king, but the witch was only the child of a woodsman and of no royal lineage. Years passed and it came time for him to choose a bride. The giant did not have the courage to speak for what he wanted so the father chose for him. Betrayed, the witch's love turned cold and she vowed revenge."

"Soon after the wedding the father died and the giant became king. The witch then turned all her fury upon him. Everything he tried fail. His wife died in childbirth. And he screamed into the starless night, 'Why?' A war came. His armies fled the field. And he screamed among their corpses, 'Why?' Treaties he made were broken. And he screamed throughout the castle, 'Why?' Crops failed. And he screamed into the fields, 'Why?' Terrible storms raged across the land for days, weeks. And he screamed and he screamed but no answer came."

"Day by day he lost hope, and day by day the witch only grew more cruel. Soon, all the people of his kingdom were either dead or emigrants. His land laid waste, he tried to kill himself, but the witch would not let him die. As her final curse she made him mad, so mad that every human being he sees he kills. Her work complete, the witch moved somewhere further north, somewhere beyond all reach where no one might break the curse. She lies in an icy cave at the top of the world, strong as the post of the earth itself, and as immovable. Her heart is still bitter, bitter and as dead as the giant is mad and forlorn."

"How can I help him then? I've come so far. You say he will kill me if he sees me?"

"He would crush you in his right hand without blinking."

"Then you must help me,' the boy said. 'I will hide beneath your belly and speak to him."

"How will that help?"

"He is mad. Why not listen to you?"

So the mouse agreed and the boy crawled beneath the mouse's belly and urged the mouse to climb to the top of the giant's shoulder. He screamed to wake the dead. But the giant went on sleeping.

The boy cupped his hands and spoke a name he had only that instant remembered.

The giant stirred. The boy spoke again. The giant sat up and shook his great matted head covering the boy and mouse in dirty, oily hair. The mouse scurried down the giant's arm afraid.

"Who's there?" the giant mumbled.

"I've come to help you," the boy answered.

"I said, Who's there?" the giant asked again, louder, anger rising in his voice. His hair and beard were so thick and bushy that the boy's small voice could not penetrate. He booted the mouse who pushed mightily to claw its way back up the giant's arm.

"You called and I came," the boy shouted.

The giant looked at the mouse and blinked stupidly.

"I called?" he squinted.

"Yes," said the boy. "you needed me. Something happened. You were lost."

"Yes," the giant sighed. "I am lost. As lost as any man. I am lost and I have lost. I have lost everything...."

The giant waved his hands into the air and slowly spread his arms, raised his chin, his face yearning into the air. His breathing sped up and tears began to flow from his dark eyes.

"In my…in my pride, in…. I…I had so much. But it was…I did not value it for what it was. I wanted…so much. I settled…I should've asked for what I wanted. It was my fear. It is so big. I had dreams. Dreams and delusions. But that is nothing. Isn't that what she told me? I am no different than anyone else. We all think we are special. We all make those decisions. When to give this up. When to know everything. When to call an act of cowardice a practical compromise. Yes, my madness, I am lost. How appropriate that a mouse speaks to me. A lion of a man. A mouse devouring me. I deserve what I get. It is the judgment of the gods. Madness then death."

"No," the boy called. "You are not being judged. You are who you are. Not special, it is true. But unique. For it was your voice and your voice only that I heard. I came from far away and long ago to help you."

"I have a sentimental madness, do I?" the giant softly laughed. "This is how I came to this, eh? Is that what you are saying? I am sorry if I have brought you here. There is no reason for you to help me. I am dying. I must die."

"But you must die differently than this. You called me. If you were dead, I would not be here."

"Who are you?"

"You know who I am. You are not mad if I am here. Put me in your pocket and keep me there for three days. On the third day send me to that place you cannot go."

"I need to know who you are," the giant sneered and picked up the mouse by its tail.

"You know so much, but you don't know who I am. I am hope no bigger than your fingernail riding on a mouse who obeys my commands. Does that help you?"

The giant scowled holding the mouse inches from his face. But he couldn't see the boy. He saw only his pain, only more evidence of his curse.

"As you say," he said flatly. "I don't need to know anymore. It wouldn't help anyway. I will take you at your word. Three days, you say? What shall I do?"

"Just put me in your pocket," the boy whispered, "and pay attention to your dreams."

"Yes," the giant answered. "I can do that. They torture me so. How could I not?"

"I will see you there. Together we will find what you need."

"As you say," sighed the giant. He put the mouse in his pocket, turned his back to the door, and curled in sleep.

The boy, too, closed his eyes. He called upon his friend the otter who best knew the realm of dreams. Otter spirit came and rolled inside the boy's soul. Soon they were in the dreams of the giant.

At first the boy could only hear groans and far away cries. The colors of groans and cries, indistinct streaks cutting across a muddy darkness. Then a whirling smoke and a faint scene, a painting unfolding in all directions.

It was a gray land. Broken columns of pink marble formed a crooked spiral stairway from the bottom of a great, treeless hill. Wisps of red clouds stretched low across a distant mountain range. A single yellow bird circled directly overhead. The otter danced along a creek that curved around the bottom of the hill; its black waters disappeared into a steaming chasm, a jagged scar that cut across the entire landscape.

The boy followed the otter to the hill and started to climb. The otter dove into the chasm and leapt out a few moments later with a sparkling salmon in its mouth. It loped ahead of the boy and waited at the top. The boy trudged up the hill, sank deeper into the earth at each step. The hill began to wobble and melt.

"Fly," the otter thought at the boy.

The boy lifted his legs at once. He floated just above the undulating earth and landed on a broken column near the very top of the hill. A white horse lay dead on a black slab of granite. Blood poured from its mouth and from a deep gash in its chest. Half-buried beside it was a silver sword, tarnished and cracked.

"What do I do?" the boy asked in a whisper.

"Feed him this." The otter dropped the salmon at the boy's feet. It floated just above the ground, swayed to and fro as if it would swim away. The boy extended his hand and the fish was in it. Its skin was iridescent and transparent. Inside it, golden pearls roiled in blue flames. The boy turned his hand slowly. The pearls fell one by one from the mouth of the fish into the wound of the horse. Soft rain began to fall.

The boy lifted his head to the sky. The bird circled closer and closer toward the top of the hill then burst into a dazzling, blinding flame. The horse rose, reared on its hind legs. Its mane was as bright as the sun.

"Time to go," the otter barked. The boy woke. He could hear the giant crying. And this time he could feel the tears.

The giant gently pressed his hand against his pocket and whispered, "Thank you, friend mouse. I feel something growing in my heart. I've not felt anything inside myself for many years. Nothing but dead things. Ghosts and cruel spirits. I've had a dead man's heart. And now I feel something again. It hurts. But it is something. The hurt is something. It is good."

The boy said nothing for a while.

"Shall we go outside?" the giant finally said. "I've not seen the sun for a long, long time." He stood and clouds of dust rose into the air, huge clods of earth tumbled to the floor from the stiffened wrinkles in his clothes. A flurry of moths flew from his frayed collar; dozens of spiders and cockroaches dropped from him and crawled hurriedly away.

The giant puffed out a small laugh. "Seems I had a kingdom after all, eh, mouse?"

The boy peered out of the pocket. "You had abandoned yourself. Welcome back!" the boy shouted.

"We'll see; we'll see," the giant snorted.

He lumbered to the door and lifted it up, placed it back on its hinges.

"There, mouse. From now on the spiders will have to knock." He smiled and stepped out into the gray cold. The sun faintly glowed through the thick cloud cover directly overhead.

"Not much of a sun, mouse. Why is it hiding?"

"There is still work to be done. We have two more nights of dreaming, remember? Yesterday there was no sign of the sun. The land was lightless."

"Lightless? Lightless. Yes, I remember."

The giant raised his hands and gazed sternly into his palms.

"I once held a golden ball," he said softly. "The years went by and covered it with shame and doubt and fear. Covered it until it was utterly black, until it sank down with its own dreadful weight and disappeared. I once held it in these same hands."

The giant stood staring at his hands for a long time. Snow began to fall again, but the giant didn't move. Slowly the day faded.

"Let's go back in," the boy gently urged as the night winds began to stir. "It's time to dream again."

The giant sighed and shook the snow from his wide shoulders. "Yes, mouse. I can still hear you," he said. "My madness has not abandoned me yet, it seems. I will do as you request."

He turned and knocked on the door. "It is me. Master of the mad house. May I come in? Yes, I may. Good. Let us now dream, my guest. Let us entertain the demons and perhaps an angel will slip in among the crowd."

The boy closed his eyes and waited for the otter to guide him into the giant's dream. But out of the dream fog a raven flew down and hopped toward him chasing a snake. The snake slithered between the boy's legs and crawled swiftly up the boy's back, becoming the boy's spine. Its head swayed above the boy's, its hood spread and tongue flashing. The raven flew up and attacked the snake with claws as big as the giant's hands and a beak like scissors. The rasping sound of the beak opening and closing terrified the boy, but the snake stiffened and raised its head higher. The boy suddenly felt braver. He became the snake, its mouth open, its fangs ready to pierce the monstrous bird. The claws of the raven became hands, strangling hands gripping the snake's throat, the boy's throat. Two new snake heads sprang from the boy's shoulders. Tongues of blue flame shot from the heads' mouths. The wings of the bird burst into flame. Metallic screams rang in the boy's ears. He opened his mouth. It was the size of a mountain. The raven fell into it, burning and screaming.

The boy turned and stood on the mountain. In the distance he saw a golden horse standing in a black river. The boy looked at his left hand. A small black snake curled in his palm. Its skin split open. Gold ribbons flowed over the boy's hand and up his arm and over his body. He felt a heat in his heart. Rays of light broke from his chest. 'The ice is melting,' someone said behind him.

He turned. A woman all in white, icy, her face pale blue, stood inside a blackberry patch. The thorns cut into her skin, but no blood flowed. She was crying silently.

The boy woke up.

"What have you done, mouse?" the giant sighed. "You've brought her back. She…she was the one. It was…. What have I done? Mouse? Mouse? What have I done?"

The boy didn't answer. The giant sat up and pulled the mouse and boy from his pocket. He held them in his hand, but didn't look at them. The boy slid from beneath the mouse and gazed up into the giant's face. Dried tears marked the giant's cheeks. His large dark eyes stared at the door.

The giant stayed inside all that day. He sat with his legs crossed. His eyes focused always on the door. The boy crawled back under the mouse who scampered down the giant's leg and into a hole in the corner of the room. "There's a few seeds for you," he said to the boy. "We need to eat. I can find some more outside."

"I'm not hungry," the boy replied. "But you go ahead. I'll watch the giant while you do whatever you have to do."

The mouse hurried down the back of the wall and outside into the snow to look for more food. The boy walked back inside the room and hid himself in some debris near the giant's litter. He sat all day watching the sad dark man stare at the door. Occasionally, the giant sighed deeply and rubbed a massive hand across his deeply furrowed brow. Other than that, he sat like a statue carved from time itself.

Dusk came and the mouse still had not returned. The boy began to worry. He crawled out of the debris and toward the mouse's hole. As he moved, he bumped into a silver button, long fallen from the giant's coat. A ray from the setting sun touched the button and the light reflected into the giant's right eye. The boy froze against the wall, trying not even to breathe.

"What's this?" the giant bellowed. He leaned over onto his hands and knees and picked up the button. He studied it closely, his face scowling as if he were trying to remember something. Then his face turned deathly white. "Her," he whispered. "On my wedding day. I betrayed her. I worried the button loose. I…I remember."

"What do you remember?" the boy suddenly asked.

"What? Mouse?" The giant squinted past the button and into the boy's eyes.

"No, it is not the mouse. He helped me. I was the one who spoke to you. I…."

But the boy could not finish his sentence. The giant snatched up the boy and jumped to his feet all at once. He roared the words, "A human," so loudly the door flew open.

And there in the doorway stood the witch glistening wet as if she had just stepped from the ocean. She stretched out her arms and an arc of light flashed from palm to palm three times then shot into the giant's heart. The giant's back arched and he dropped the boy into the pile of rags he'd used as a bed. Light shot from his fingertips and his head was shrouded in flames. He opened his mouth and a gold liquid rainbowed through the room and into face of the witch. The shack trembled and the timbers burst apart as if pulled by a tornado sent by the gods themselves.

The boy covered his eyes as a brilliant golden light swirled in from all directions, even from inside the earth itself. He heard a rasping sound and opened his eyes in terror expecting to see the horrible raven. But the sound came from a huge gold door opening to reveal a crowd of people cheering in a courtyard, the sun shining brilliantly down upon them. The sky was bright blue. The scent of fruit blossoms filled the air. The giant and the witch dressed in royal finery stood in the doorway waving to the crowd.

The couple turned to face the boy. The giant smiled at him and then looked at the witch, his eyes soft as tears of joy freely streamed down his cheeks.

"Why did you come back?" he whispered.

"I came back because of him," she said. "He saved you and he saved me. He saved us. Your hope saved us. The curse is lifted. We have been restored."

The witch walked to the boy and lifted him gently into the palm of her hand. "Bless you, boy. Your dreaming is beyond all magic I have known. You lifted the shadow from me. Thank you. Whatever I can do for you, I will."

"You listened. You allowed yourself to be seen," the boy answered. "That is more than enough."

"Why did you help me?" the giant asked.

"Does it matter?" the boy replied.

"I asked myself everyday since I lost my kingdom," the giant said. "Yet, I suppose you are right. Asking didn't help much."

"You called and I came to help you,' the boy smiled, "not because of why, but because you hadn't lost hope. I waited in the blackberry patch where you had abandoned me until you knew what was truly important."

"I did not abandon you. I do not know you. What did I know that was important?" The giant frowned.

"There are things we put aside without remembering why. There are places in our hearts that never forget. We are not small or poor in the greater world if we recognize the wonders we have hidden in our dreams. All we need to do is open our eyes and see, and be seen, for who we are. Goodbye, my giant friend; my lady. My old friends miss me in the blackberry patch."

"I'll plant you a blackberry patch!" The giant exclaimed.

"Thank you, but I miss my friends. If you need me, just call. I'll see you in your dreams. After all, I still owe you one. Now I must find my way back home."

"I will take care of that, my young friend," the witch said. She raised her right hand and turned it slowly. Colored ribbons of light tumbled into the air.

A giant raven flew down from a golden tower of the giant's renewed castle. "Thank you, my lady," the boy said as he jumped on the raven's back. The raven hopped once and took to the sky, circled twice as the boy waved goodbye to the giant and his new bride, and then disappeared into the clouds.

***

Jill threw a handful of powder into the fire sending crackling streamers of color spiraling into the night—elemental dragons taking to the air.

Jack smiled tightly, wanting to cry, and looked out to the ocean. Several dolphins leaped from a moon mirror shimmering on the water.

"There seem to be fish in many of your stories," he whispered, clearing his throat to choke the tears.

"Fish are dreams," she smiled. "Dreams abandoned, dreams to come, dreams unwanted, dreams needed to feed the soul. There used to be so many fish in the sea. Now I hear many are on the verge of extinction. To think that could happen is beyond my imagination. But I am told it is true. And I wonder if our dreams, too, have been diminished? Everyone with the same dream, dreams formed in some factory, on some computer program.

A menu of dreams instead of an overflowing cornucopia. So many people giving up their dreams…out…of some fear? Fear of what, do you think?"

"Uncertainty?" Jack shrugged. "I don't know. Dreams are so slippery."

"Yes, yes they are," she said. "But without them we eat and sleep and die in a wasteland. Dead horses on a gray abandoned hill. A hollow echo forever screaming, 'Why, why, why?' So sad to never seek the black waters where the dreams wait. Love and longing need no proof, need no gods or mystery larger than themselves, larger than the one hand helping another. Uncertainty, indeed. So sad."

Jill rose and walked toward the ocean.

Jack sat for a long time staring into the fire. When he looked up she was gone. He followed her footsteps to the surf and looked up and down the beach. He knew she had gone back to the tower.

He walked back to the fire. Reaching into his pocket, he pulled out the rosewood box with the scarf inside. For a few minutes, he stared at it, then tossed it onto the fire and walked away.

The Golden Ball

He drove away from the beach regretting the day he'd met her. When the box caught fire he'd wished he'd placed every single day he'd known her inside of it. Every day he'd thought about her, dreamed about her, even the days before he'd actually set eyes upon her. How big a box for that? For a day? For an hour? How many cubic feet does a minute take up? Particular minutes? Some in the eye of a gnat, some perhaps in the Pyramid of Cheops? How big a box to burn away years of turning around waiting to see her come around that corner?

He didn't stop driving until the sun came up. A few hours after he left the beach he stopped outside of Needles for gas, but he didn't remember it until the bill came three weeks later.

The night was a blur, as empty of memories as the desert sky was full of stars.

Pain. An aching like poison knotting in the belly. There was that, a timeless eternity of that. But that wasn't a memory. That was merely his condition: A hollowed ache with a headlights' sheen driving into the myriad constellations written on every night's lost face. Her face. A billion versions of her face.

His thoughts wound wide and looping and ever down, spiraling down, circling a place he knew he had to enter, a place darker than his courage would ever allow him to go. He had talked to people about this place. They had asked for his help. He was known as a wise fellow, someone who dispensed practical advice that didn't demean fear or lessen the reality of failure. But he always knew there was one place beyond advice. No one can tell you how to deal with that particular problem. Certainly the advice might be precise, might actually work, but that wasn't the issue. The issue was this: There is no hell like the one in your own heart. That hell was made of a darkness specific to your character. It knew all your tricks, all your evasions, all your shameful tactics to keep yourself safe. How do you outsmart yourself? How do you forget the necessary lies?

Back and forth. Back and forth. Rocking to a silent music. A space between. Looking for the space, the thin place that only grace would provide. Something to drive him. A place to go where things were bright and clear. Clarity. All he wanted was a clear point of departure. A place to begin. A place to begin again. He was caught in a loop. A black hole. Timeless. He began to hallucinate. A blaring horn woke him. It was dawn.

He pulled over somewhere in the middle of New Mexico to get some gas and use the facilities. The place was closed. The sign said they'd be open at 6:00. He checked to see if there was an automated pump. No luck. He tried the bathroom door. Naturally, it was locked. He walked around back and headed a few yards into the sagebrush, relieved himself, and then simply stood gazing at the orange-tinged distant hills until his eyelids grew heavy and he began to sway with the rising wind. A face. The wind, a face just like in the Greek stories. A face of liquid air. White and blue and clear. Formed just at the beginning of things. The first thing. A breath. A face formed by breath. Only it was a woman's face. Not hers, but another's. A beautiful, lonely face. Something brushed his leg while heading back toward the station.

Wide awake. He turned and scanned the ground. Animal tracks. He ran out of the brush. A white coyote limped across the blacktop, beyond his Jeep, and into the brush. The animal shot a glance at him just before it disappeared. It took his breath away. Tears rushed up from the tightness of his chest and streamed from his burning eyes. He fell to his knees, buried his face in his hands, crumbled.

"I'm...losing my mind," he whispered, breathless, into the red earth. "Simply losing...my mind."

"You okay, mister?"

The voice jerked him upright, his hands raised to ward off an invisible evil.

A young boy in overalls and a straw hat stared warily at him.

He looked at the boy for a few seconds, unsure if the boy was another hallucination. He blinked a few times, twisted his shoulders, both to feel the tightness of real muscles and to make it seem like he was simply doing his morning exercises. If the boy was real, he didn't want the boy telling about some weird man crying in the field behind a gas station.

"Uh, just, you know, waiting for the station to open. Needed to relieve myself. You know, potty. Stretch a bit. You know? I'm fine. Just been driving. Long way. Really tired. Uh, where'd you come from?"

"I live around here. Where did you come from?" the boy answered, still looking a bit suspicious.

"Long way. Ocean."

"Ocean? Which one?"

"Yeah, right. Which one? The Pacific. What, you think I could've made it in a night from the Atlantic?"

"Beats me. Why would you want to do that anyway?" the boy asked, scowling at the man like he wasn't going to be taken for a fool.

"Indeed, kid. Listen. When does the station open? My watch says 5:30 so I was thinking it should be open now."

"Dudn't open till it supposed to."

"Right. But like I said, my watch says 5:30 and that's Pacific time."

"Time's all the same," the boy shrugged.

"Right. Okay. Do you know where the owner lives?"

"Nobody owns time."

"No, no. The owner of the station."

The boy pointed to his left. "Lives that way."

"Well, that…uh…listen. Do you know the owner?"

"Yes," the boy said. He moved to his right, squatted in the dirt, and started poking at the tracks on the ground.

The man covered his face exasperated. "Do you think you could…."

The boy stood back up and said, "What's your name?"

"Uh…Jack. Jack Jilson," he lied.

"Well, Jack. You look like you lost something."

He studied the boy's face searching for…what? His shoulders ached. He rolled them and turned away. Guileless the boy might be, still he wanted something else. Something simpler than a boy, simpler than…. "Oh, Christ, kid. Yeah. Yeah, I did lose something," he suddenly said.

"What? What was it?" the boy challenged.

"Oh, hell. I don't know."

"Then how do you know you lost it?"

Jack knelt and lifted the boy's chin with the tips of his fingers.

"How old are you?" Jack asked.

"Eight. That's old."

"Yeah, well it's old enough to know when one's being a smarty."

"I'm not being a smarty. How do you know what you've lost if you can't name it?"

"You know," Jack mumbled. "The thing. The spirit of…it…it's…"

"I know what you mean if you're saying you don't know where you lost it."

"Well," Jack frowned and stood up again. "I don't really know what or where or..."

"Then you're crazy," the boy said matter-of-factly.

"Yeah. Geez, kid. That's exactly what I think it is."

"Like a coyote, though, right?" the boy suddenly asked whispering, edging in closer to Jack, looking a little lost himself.

"Coyotes aren't crazy," Jack smiled.

"Then why do they howl at the moon? People say you're crazy when you howl at the moon like a coyote. Is that because you're telling your enemies where you are, acting crazy and all. Somebody can shoot you when they know where you are."

Jack squinted at the boy. This was a strange conversation. He wondered if the boy's father was a drinker. The father had probably run into a little trouble. He sighed. The world spun its stories out and out, relentlessly. Here he had run to the middle of nowhere and found a boy as deep into the drama of life as anyone else he knew. He smiled to himself. It was a gift, this boy's troubles. Made his craziness seem indulgent.

"Can we go sit in the front?" Jack asked. "My back is kinda sore and those chairs I saw looked comfortable."

"Sure," the boy shrugged and turned to go, but spun back almost immediately, his eyes wide and he blurted out in one breath. "But ya hav'ta tell me what ya know about the coyote."

"Sure, sure," Jack nodded. "Just as soon as we sit down." He sighed as he tried to put his right hand on the boy's shoulder, but the boy slid out from his touch and walked a few paces ahead of him.

They walked to the front of the station. A white tin roof covered the store entrance and extended out several yards to the single set of pumps. Next to the drink machine by the black-gated door two metal lawn chairs were turned backwards to the wall. Their lime green paint had peeled up in the heat, forming a regular pattern of almost perfect triangles spaced an inch or so apart. Combined with the rusting circular rivets, the effect was of feathers or a fungal fur, the skin of a bizarre creature with golden rusty spots.

But the chairs looked sturdy enough for Jack's back. He flipped one around and sighed deeply as he eased into the contoured seat. The boy just stood right in front of Jack waiting patiently for him to stop wriggling and start talking. Jack chuckled at the boy's impatience. Who exactly was the youngster here? Jack finally leaned over and flipped the other chair.

"You gonna sit?" he asked the boy.

"Don't wanna sit. It's daylight," the boy answered studying something crawling on the wall. He slapped at it. "Hate bugs," he sneered at the yellow stain in his palm. The death stank. "Go wipe it in the dirt, boy," Jack said whiffing the air with his hat. The boy bent down and rubbed his hand in a tuft of rye grass growing from the cracks of the concrete where the garage met the store.

Jack shrugged, turned to the east. He stared across a hard packed lot stained with oil and other colored liquids dripped from the innards of broken cars. But those vehicles were ghosts, as were the owners: tourists, farmers, honeymooners, angry wives on the way to Vegas to get a divorce, hitchhikers, sleepy truckers, salesmen wondering why they lost that last sale, why they ever thought they could make a sale, lonely men and women just driving on and on into the night looking for a desire that they couldn't even name.

He imagined two old wrecked trucks as people. They were dressed in black, faceless; their heads bowed underneath the sun, strange people from another dimension waiting for a bus that never came, or they were old people in a home waiting forever for a visitor, any visitor; turning to each other in their forlorn loneliness. They were young lovers with old souls holding hands on a cliffside, stepping off. They were simply the blinding light of the morning.

The sun was fully up now, a brilliant golden ball blazing in a cloudless blue sky. The color reminded him of the edges of his mother's plates when he was a boy. Something Dutch. Ice blue. Cold. Skating along a silver sea. Hans Brinker. The color of courage.

"It's a beautiful sky for a boy," he finally said as he turned his gaze back to the kid. "One could imagine anything happening up there in that kind of sky. Magical. Warplanes, spaceships, pirates."

The youngster seemed completely uninterested in Jack's speech. A few uncomfortable seconds passed before Jack felt compelled to look to the sky again.

"The storms must be magnificent, too," he offered. "Do you like it when the rains come?"

"Can't play outside when it rains, mister," the kid smirked. He stepped out from under the overhang and looked straight up into the sky.

"Buzzards," he said shading his eyes. "Must be something dead or dying. Buzzards like the sky when it's clear like this." He stepped back into the shade and continued his disconcerting stare. "You gonna tell me why coyotes howl at the moon or not?"

Jack was getting a headache. He leaned forward a little and turned just slightly to look inside the store. Pain was getting to him. Felt old, so old.

"You know if they have any aspirin in there?"

"I don't know," the boy mumbled.

"Don't know or don't know where?" Jack grinned.

"Now who's being a smarty?" the kid challenged, but this time his tongue stuck out just a bit. He couldn't contain a sly smile.

"Well," Jack asked nodding again at the window, "do they? Can you get in there?"

"No."

"Damn," Jack grimaced. "Not even a broken window? A broken lock?" The boy mute. Jack scratched at his temples with both hands. "Man, I have a headache."

"Well, I can do something for that," the young one sniffed and spun on his bare heels and walked off toward the lot.

"Really?" Jack called after him.

"Sure." The boy skipped into a run and ran to the nearest wrecked truck. He stooped next to the driver's side door. He reached under the chassis. Twisting his neck around, he grunted a few times. Obviously whatever he was after was deeper underneath than the boy had remembered. He finally lay on his belly and stuck his head under the truck. A wriggle or two and all you could see were the black, bare soles of the boy's feet. A few seconds later he wriggled backwards, pulled himself out with a loud "hmpf," and came running all proud back to Jack.

"This'll work for headaches," he puffed.

He held out a wrinkled brown paper bag to Jack with one hand and brushed off the front of his overalls with the other.

Jack took it gingerly from the beaming boy and immediately could tell by the weight what it was.

"Whiskey?" He raised the bottle to his nose and sniffed at the cap, grinned at the boy who was rubbing his freckled nose with the inside of his bird-thin wrist. "You don't drink this stuff, do you?" Jack teased.

The kid sniffed a few times at the air craning his neck from side to side as if to drain his sniffles down one nostril or the other. "No, sir," he coughed. "I don't drink none of that. But Grandpa says it is very good for headaches in the morning. Maybe if I ever get a headache I'll take some, but my head never hurts. Just get the sniffles and drainage. Hate that drainage, but don't get no headaches."

"Lucky you," Jack sighed, watching a little clear line roll from a nostril to the top of the boy's lip. He gestured to the boy with a nod of his head and a snort. "Wipe there, boy."

"Thanks," the boy said wiping again with the inside of his wrist.

"And your grandpa," Jack continued as he studied the bottle of whiskey. "He…he is a wise man, I'm sure, when it comes to headaches. This…this will certainly have to do. Hmm, but maybe with a Coke, eh? Do you drink Coke?"

"This is an RC machine."

"Well, Coke, RC, Pepsi. Don't matter. You drink cola, right? Here. How much is it?" He pulled a pocketful of change from his watch pocket and held it out for the boy.

"I don't know," the kid smirked and turned to look at the wrecks.

Jack stared at the boy and wanted to strangle him.

"Kids," he whispered. "No, not how much is this, how much is the soda. Just take what you need and buy me and you a soda."

The boy didn't even turn. He just waved his hand, shooing an invisible something toward the cars, and said, "You do it. I'm not thirsty."

Jack shook his head slightly and leaned to look at the machine.

"Fifty cents. Cheap. Great. Two quarters. Will you just take the quarters?" He whistled at the boy. The boy looked back and Jack pressed his palm close to the boy's face.

"Why don't you just drink it like Grandpa does?" the boy complained. "Just sip it from the bottle. Slow, like he says to. Says, 'slow slow and the steady grows.' That's what he says. 'Slow slow.' Always telling me that."

"Yeah, your grandpa's probably right about that. Yeah, yeah. A wise man to go slow.

Jack looked at the coins in his hand and rubbed his tongue against his teeth. He leaned to his left and let the coins slip out of his hand and back into his regular pocket.

"Pants too tight," he mumbled, then said louder. "Besides, I don't need any refined sugars today. Just some fine…uh…some regular…old…cheap…whiskey." He looked at the bagged bottle distastefully imaging the old man's hungover lips slobbering on its filthy mouth. Ah, he thought, but alcohol would kill whatever that old man might have deposited on the bottle, whatever stinky old bug he might have caught in his nightly crawls through that roadhouse, undoubtedly somewhere over those eastern hills.

Jack twisted the black, bent cap off the bottle and took a slow sip, fighting the wince that gripped his face for all of two seconds.

"That's how Grandpa looks," the boy crowed. "You'll be fine in no time. So tell me about the coyote."

"Ah, geez, boy," Jack coughed. "Your grandpa is…." He cleared his throat a couple of times. "He's a strong old man, isn't he. Skin like a rattler's, I bet."

"He hates rattlers. Won't even wear their skins. Just shoots 'em and lets the ants and lizards eat the meat. If coyotes aren't crazy," the boy said without a pause between the subjects, "why ask to be killed? Why do they come around here? They gotta know they'll get shot eventually. Ain't that crazy? Going to a place over and over until you get shot?"

"That's just life, kid. Like breathing. You just keep breathing until one day you don't. Why do it at all when you know one day it'll stop?"

"That's stupid," the boy said and spit.

Jack laughed out loud. "Yeah, you're right, kid. That's philosophy with its head up its ass. Pardon my French."

"So, will you be quiet about that other stuff now and talk about the coyote?"

"Jab. Jab." The boy's brazenness amused Jack. He wondered if he could be that direct with people. And then he said aloud, "If only I could be that direct with myself."

"Your head is moving like a puppet. Who's pulling on ya?"

"You're a funny little boy, you know that? Reminds me of…of how it could be."

"Is that good?" Hunched shoulders told Jack the boy didn't think it was good.

"It's not a matter of good. It is.... I'm not making fun of you. Not really making myself clear. I'm just not around kids much. I like you. I think...I know I can learn a lot from you. Not how to be a kid, but how to be more of who I am. I'm not one of those guys who thinks the end-all and be-all of being human is being a kid. Every age has its points. Hell, you don't even know what I'm talking about, which is one reason I'm glad I'm not a kid anymore, but there is a...a something about you. A surety. Of course, you aren't sure of anything that is important for doing, you know, things like investing bonds or engineering a power plant, but there's a.... You just do what you do and...it's right for you."

"And you are crazy because you say you lost something but you don't even know what it is and you're talking to a kid?" The boy lifted his chin like a cocky fighter, flared his narrow nostrils, daring Jack to take the challenge.

"Yeah," Jack heckled back. "I lost something and it makes me sad. What's so crazy about that?" He took another swig from the bottle. His mouth didn't twist away from it this time. He snorted in and hocked out a copper colored nut of spit.

"You don't know what you lost which means maybe it wasn't yours to lose," the boy replied hotly and spat at the same spot. Dogs marking territory.

"Look, kid." Jack was getting tired of this. The irritation showed in the deepening of his voice, the disappearance of any sing-song inflection. This was straight talk now, the voice of free breathing; no one left to impress. Just you and that other set of human eyes, a humanity ageless, genderless, cultureless. Raw. Revealed. Everyone can get to that point if they want to. Like there's a switch somewhere just behind the eyes. A two-year-old can be there as well as the most obstinate fool. There's a tone to it. It ends the game. Cuts through politics, religious factionalism, sexist palaver. We can all do it. And there's usually two or three times in our lives when we do. Doesn't last long, usually. Sometimes less than an inhale and an exhale. But it is a true moment. As true as anything human can be. An exchange takes place. It cuts beyond personality, beyond life itself to that place where we came from, the place where it all came from. It's that unnameable secret we all share, and all refuse to believe, except in that split second exchange. Except in the midst of a nightmare or a miracle. But those times we are alone. Being alone lessens the impact. It might have been an hallucination. When you look into another's eyes and that knowledge arcs between you, there is no disguise to take to the face of it. No shame to hide behind, no fear to run to. No reasoning to calculate into insignificance.

"You ever lose something?" Jack asked.

"Yes." The boy said it slowly, calmly. The voice of an angel at a tribunal in hell. All eyes trained on him. Condemned before time began. But his back is erect. His chest is out and relaxed. Breathing in and out.

"What was it?" Jack snapped, leaning into the air from the bow of a speeding cloud.

"My mother."

Jack froze.

Everything stopped.

The wind that had been rising with the sun suddenly stilled. There had been a hum of insects, the calling of distant crows, the creaks and whistlings of the telephone poles that lined both sides of the highway, the drone of the cola machine, the rub of Jack's weight on the metal chair. All cut out at just that moment. And a cloud, invisible a mere second before, gasped into existence above the eastern horizon, instantly softening the light as if the sun had narrowed its eye, stunned again by old news. We know. We know so much. We know the truth. We know the intimate details. Yet, still, every time we hear, we can't believe it. And we know that even the sun, older than the earth, is ever shocked by the news, though it turns and turns and turns and has seen it all. We know that, too, though we claim it isn't true. The world is alive. The sun and moon and even old wrecks. They witness. Only they don't speak. They have too much respect to speak. And in moments like this moment, everyone knows what the connection really is. The necessary lies fall away, the veil is pulled up, and the clarity of it all snaps its fearsome and loving mouth to ours and sucks out our breath just like....

And as fast as its gone, the light changes back.

The sounds return. The veil falls down again. We breathe in...and out.

"I'm so sorry," Jack said as if waiting for his cue from the sun. "I...when did she...?"

"She went crazy and killed herself," the boy shrugged.

"Oh, my god."

"S'okay," the boy said. "She was really crazy. Not like you. You're just stupid crazy. She was sad crazy. Grandpa says for sad-crazy people it's okay to die young, to die before their time. Said people like her were more afraid of living than dying so it was okay. Grandpa says only stupid people don't run away from what really scares 'em."

"I don't know if that's true, son," Jack whispered.

"Well," the boy said slowly. He thought about it for awhile, chewed on his thumbnail and stared at the ground without blinking. Jack noticed all the boy's nails were short. People who chew on their nails worry on the inside. Attack themselves instead of defending themselves from aggression. Jack was like that. Thinking about it, he began to chew on a thumbnail himself.

"I don't know," the boy finally said. "But it sure is hard not to run when you're really scared. We found her at the bottom of the canyon. Coyotes were beside her, guarding her like. They only ran away when we got right up on them and grandpa shot his gun in the air. There were bugs all over her. Ants and…I hate bugs." His voice trailed off and Jack couldn't understand what he said.

Jack lowered his head and didn't look at the boy. He didn't even want to breathe. The paper on the bottle crinkled and Jack squeezed it again as if it would quieten through brute force. He sighed.

"So you were with them?" he asked, clearing his throat. "At the canyon?" He took another swig and offered the bottle to the boy.

The boy frowned.

"Oh, yeah. Right. Sorry," Jack hemmed. "Just, it seemed like."

"It's okay," the boy smiled. "Grandpa forgets, too. He…uh…actually made me take a swallow of that in the canyon. I guess I even wanted to. But, it don't taste good. It didn't seem…."

"Yeah," Jack smiled back. "Adults forget. But, you said the coyotes were guarding her? How many? Did that bother you?"

The boy's mood instantly changed with the mention of the coyotes. Jack straightened up. Stood up and pulled the coins back out. He walked to the cola machine and pressed the RC button. A loud series of clankings delivered a cold can with a thud into the receiving bin.

"Want one?" Jack called loud enough for the ghosts to hear it in the wrecks. He suddenly stopped and faced the boy.

"You know, I don't know your name. You have a name, yes?"

"Well, Grandpa calls me Willie though that ain't what nobody else calls me. But you can call me Willie cause, well, just cause. And I'd take an RC. Not a diet one. Mama said sugar's at least real and if you're gonna get fat anyway you might as well get fat on real."

"Amen to that, Willie," Jack shouted.

He pressed the RC button and another one flew down the clanky channels. Jack sat back down, popped one for Willie and handed it to him, then popped his own, poured out about half of it onto the ground and said, "To old diabetics." He filled the can with whiskey, raised the can high and drank deep. "RC and whiskey. Feel like a brand new man."

The boy shook his head, grinning, and waving Jack off. "You ain't brand new. You're just getting drunk. It ain't even eight o'clock."

"Damn, you may be right," Jack laughed. "I don't think I've ever drunk this early before. A girlfriend's uncle got me snockered on homemade brandy once. Eleven in the morning. He kept pouring it into a shot glass. By the time the girlfriend's old man showed up to pick us up I was three sheets to the wind. That one didn't last."

Jack looked back to the west. He took a smaller sip from the can. "I didn't know you weren't supposed to drink it all. The trick is to keep just a little in the glass. If you drain it, the host feels he has to fill it up."

He looked at the boy who just stood there studying Jack's face. "Hmm. I thought I learned that then, but maybe...maybe I didn't. What do you think, Willie? Have I been drinking things up too fast? Not paying attention?"

"Well, you did lose that thing that you lost," Willie said, his voice slowing. Tears welled in his eyes and his lower lip began to tremble. Jack noticed the quivering of the boy's belly. Deep sobs boiling in the belly. Jack felt them bubbling in his own belly.

"No, Willie, no. It wasn't your fault, Willie. It wasn't anyone's fault. I know what you're thinking, what you're feeling, and I'm not telling you not to feel that way. You can't help the way you feel, but believe me it wasn't your fault. It's just that you miss her. And I'm sure she misses you. It's not what you think. The sadness isn't blaming you, Willie. It's trying to release you.

He gazed up into the sky, squinting into the brilliance of that singular star.

"You know, the heart is a lot like the sun. You know? A golden ball, full of energy. That's what your heart is. But things happen to it. You ever hear of spots on the sun? Sun spots? Kind of black places? Well, in your life there are things that happen to you. Disappointments. People leave. People are cruel. Say mean things, do mean things. And these are like black spots. They begin to stick to your heart."

He rubbed his thumb over the mouth of the can and smiled softly.

"Years go by and the energy of your heart, that golden ball of energy, gets dimmer and dimmer. Those black spots are like the tarry oil stains on that lot over there. Each time a bad thing happens, the tar gets thicker. Eventually, the golden ball seems to disappear under all that blackness. You forget you ever had a golden ball for a heart."

He winced and looked away from the boy. He wasn't about to cry. This was hard, he thought. Why is this so hard?

"I think that's what happened to me. Maybe that's what I lost. I lost the memory of that golden ball. But you know, I think I know how to get it back. I think it's about being sad. I think being sad is a good thing if it makes you start to dig into that tar, makes you start digging away at it. It's hard, of course. It hurts. Even scary. But you can't run away from it. You can't, because if you do, you'll never know that gold, that gold that was once there.

"The first wound is to the heart. But it's not just you. We are all wounded. The golden ball is buried in the wound. And I think the sadness is the way to get at it, but I can't really tell you how to dig, Willie. No one can tell you how to dig. No one can speak to the fear you have as you dig your tunnel through the tar. That's your own hell, my young friend. Every path is different; every path scary in its own peculiar way. But if you have the courage to dig, you will find golden sparks."

Jack cleared his throat and took a small swig. He smiled up at the sun.

"The sadness is trying to release you from your mother's death. You still have that golden ball in you. It has a few spots, but it's trying to shake them off before they become so tarry that you have to wait till you're my age to learn what a wonderful thing a heart is. Hold that sadness, but don't get stuck in it? Okay? It's not your fault."

Willie started to cry, to sob. He dropped his soda and buried his face in his hands.

"Yes, that's good," Jack whispered. "The tears help wash that blackness away. It makes the heart shine. Shine as bright as the sun. A great golden ball of a sun. Cry, Willie. Don't ever let anyone tell you not to cry."

Jack stood and walked to the boy, put out his hand, but Willie looked up and shook his head no.

"It's okay. Cry like you cry. It's your heart. Feel what you feel. I'll be over here in the chair. Just cry. I'll be here."

Jack sat back down and closed his eyes. He thought about her. Wondered how he could ever have been so wrong. It was her speaking when he told Willie that story. As he talked, he could see her, feel her voice playing into his bones. Only she told the story about a girl. About herself. And as she told it, it was him telling her. Only he was old. A grandfather telling his grandchild a story. Stories within stories. Hearts within hearts. The sun has seen so many stories told. Over and over. And each one told the story of the sun itself. The golden ball covered in blackness and returning again. Childhood to old age to childhood. One madness to another. A wonderful, divine madness of the heart. The heart waiting to be seen.

When he opened his eyes, the sun was directly overhead. Willie was gone. So was the bag with the whiskey in it. The RC can lay on the ground beside his chair. He picked it up. Empty.

A pickup truck pulled up in front of the station and stopped on the highway. The driver called out to Jack.

Jack couldn't hear what the man was saying so he got up and walked over to the truck on the passenger side.

"Hi." Jack nodded and touched the brim of his hat.

The man in the truck shook his head in mild amusement.

Jack pulled his hat a little further down on his brow and muttered, "Just waiting for the owner to open up. Need gas."

"Well," the man said spitting out some juice from his chew, "you gonna be waitin' a long time. This station's closed. Has been for a year. I can give ya enough gas to get to Magdalena."

"Closed? But I…."

"You want the gas or not?"

"Yeah. Sure. I just…."

The man gave Jack a look and turned up the radio. He got out of his truck, picked up a five-gallon gas can and walked over to Jack's car without a glance at Jack. He popped the gas cap and poured the gas in. When he finished he walked back to where Jack still stood at the passenger door.

"Seen any coyotes?" the man asked.

"Yeah, one."

"Limping?"

"Yeah, why?"

"Oh, I'll get her. She keeps coming around, but I'll get her."

He spit again, got in his truck, and drove off.

Jack stood watching the man's truck until it disappeared in the heat waves. He walked back to the RC machine and put in two quarters. They fell through to the coin return slot.

He got in his Jeep and sat there. A tumbleweed rolled across the lot and lodged underneath one of the wrecks, the one where Willie had retrieved the bottle. Jack smiled and turned the ignition. As he pulled onto the highway the white coyote ran from behind the back of the station. Trotting behind it was a pup. It stopped for a second and looked directly at Jack. It raised its snout in the air and gave a yip, then disappeared into the brush.

The Tiger

And it all falls apart. A Humpty Dumpty jigsaw explosion rains terror from the clouds in a slow motion silent newsreel that loops through your soul forever and forever. You reach out to stop it. But the timing is just off. Always just off. Your extended hand freezes inches away. Always your mouth open and nothing coming out. The screams huddled all terrified inside.

So no one hears. And no one can help.

And everything you value dies with your silent assent.

The tiger loosed upon the world and no one notices a difference, its roarings in the streets of the city's foggy night just another siren call.

Of course, there are signs in the mists of every breakdown. There always are. They're everywhere: in the newspaper headlines, the weather's quirks gone quirkier. The portents smirk at you in the muffled neighbors' squabbles, in the just-missed phone calls, the cable failures, the lost receipts, the low memory disconnects, the tumbling, spirit breaking rolls of miscues, missteps, misunderstandings in even the most amazingly simple of transactions.

But in the hammering moments leading up to the fall, you keep turning your head just so, just a little to the left, to the right, not wanting to let the neck be twisted completely around, not wanting to hear the snap of certainty. You turn away. Imagine the signs suspended in a timeless space. You turn the signs slowly. A roasted, trichinosis-ridden pig burning above a colorless void. And in the turning, the signs grunt both yes and no.

Like the ancient frog-voiced and mumbling Grecian oracles groaning from the hot, smoke-filled caves of Delphi, the signs point right and left, up and down. The connecting arcs bridge neither true nor false. They spiral into and out of themselves, palming a wiggling mass of possibilities, a snake pit of conflicting desires and repulsions.

You're bound hand and foot. Hung from meat hooks on breathing black walls. Naked. Stuck. Utterly helpless. No logic, no faith. Beyond redemption or grace. The prophetesses howl up their helpers. Spirits whisk past you, laughing, sneering, smugly smiling, sad as orphans, blank.

They assail you endlessly. Angels, vixens, sprites. Skeletal phantasms of rotting flesh and sex-drenched loins ache through you. Leave you, for all that, empty.

Welcome to Hell: The Gateway to Heaven. Or is that backwards?

Where are the gates of hell?

Open your mouth.

But first there are just signs. Mere moments that bring a slight twitch to the cheek, a narrowing of the eyes, a nicking scratch in the throat, coy jerk of the head. Something just off center. A millimeter in the eye contact, a notch lower in the voice. A caress released just short. A subtle changing of the subject and a sigh of disinterest. One less touch in greeting, in parting. A little bit of sharpness towards your once endearing peccadilloes.

Something is withheld. Not much. But was that the first time? Or has it been a little each day for the last couple of days? Did it start at the party? That one night after making love in the inn by the lake?

Something withdrawing, drawing into itself. Away.

Closing.

Closing in.

And then things fall apart.

The gods look out and they see prisoners, psychic hostages locked away in the corners of your soul, locked away for years without light or the voice of kindness.

"Strife," they say, "is where the juice of life hides. The pearl is in the rub before the swine."

And so one day the gates, built year after year by a collusion of parental order and your need for external approval, are blasted down. The prisoners run screaming from their cells. They are in no mood for compromising uncertainty. They want to be heard and they could give a care for niceties or schedules or the economics of social emotion. They want voice. They want that thing that kept them in the dark to be destroyed, eviscerated, vaporized, gone.

They want things to fall apart.

They want things to fall apart, because things had tried to kill them.

It's as simple as that.

They say just before a suicide finally pulls the trigger, things are looking up, never looked better—as if the burning desire of the prisoners rises in a spring fever to give the suicidal that needed shot of liberating exuberance, fire them with the vital energy to do the killing deed. Or perhaps it is just one last mocking rebuke of the chains that can't be cut.

Chained to the past, and the tiger loosed upon the world.

Jack knew this. He'd tried to cut the chains, set the prisoners free.

"You don't try. You do or you don't." A neuro-linguistic certainty.

"There is no center," he wrote from the hospital, "no turning point where falling is rising. Ordinary direction, dimension become insignificant conceptions. Exploding, imploding. No difference. The new four dimensions consist only of down and black and a twisting that never stops."

Fallen apart. Jack had fallen apart and was only just pulling himself back together when he stumbled into the towered cottage and met her. She was hope. Hope and love. The only enemies of things falling apart.

But then the tornado came. She left the tower and stepped outside into the light.

The light became more frightening than the darkness of his mad cave.

His loneliness was overwhelming.

What if he really were responsible for the yearnings in his heart?

The water pump in his Jeep broke two hours after he left the gas station where he'd had the strange conversation with the coyote boy. A half hour passed before someone stopped and asked if he needed help. Another hour crawled by getting to a phone that worked.

"No towers anywhere around here, bud. Sorry."

AAA said it would take at least three hours for them to get a truck to tow him. It being Sunday and all, it'd be Monday before they could even see if they had the right pump. There was a motel about fifteen miles south. Probably be best that he check in there and call them in the morning.

The tow truck driver said he had another call but Jack could ride along and he'd drop him off at the motel since the call was close by.

It was six in the afternoon by the time Jack stepped out of the truck and onto the deserted, sand-covered parking lot of the single story, white claptrap project someone called a motel. Late as it was, the temperature still had to be near 100. Sweat poured off him like he was a roasting pig.

He stalked up to the window of the night clerk's office and slapped the buzzer. The harshness of the sound made him wince. No one stirred in the tiny room. A fist of hot sand blasted the back of his neck. He spun around ready to pound something. But it was just the wind, the swirling hot, desert winds. He wondered how many years it would take before the place drowned in the dry white grit thrown from the distant western dunes.

He slapped the buzzer again and again. His frustration rose incrementally as the perspiration dropped more quickly from the tip of his nose, from his chin, his earlobes. Beads of sweat. Cursing beads. Maybe he'd scream until someone came to his rescue or his vocal chords gave out.

His jaw hurt from grinding his teeth by the time the door of the room closest to the office opened, and a pimply teenaged girl sauntered out. An unlit cigarette dangled limply from her lips.

"Almost in the nick of time," Jack fumed, taking a quick step toward her. He took a deep breath, getting ready to blow her to Phoenix.

Then he noticed her belly. She was pregnant, very pregnant.

"Sorry," the girl said sleepily. "I was taking a nap. I get so sleepy."

"It's okay," he mumbled. "I'm sure you need the rest. I just…Well, it sure is hot and I'm really quite…."

"Yeah, it is hot. You need a room?" She didn't look at him as she unlocked the door to the clerk's office and slowly, painfully sat on a rickety metal kitchen chair. She sat for a few seconds, breathing heavily. Jack sensed it wasn't the weight of her swollen body that caused her to breathe so wearily.

"Miss…?" he whispered.

"Yes," she said. But it wasn't Jack she spoke to. She rubbed her belly then pulled the guest register from the top drawer of an unpainted desk.

"Single? Non-smoking?" she asked rummaging through the drawer for a pen.

Jack didn't answer right away. His stomach knotted and he felt like he was going to cry. She found a pen and started to write. It didn't work. She made small circles on the edge of the register until the ink began to flow.

Jack covered his mouth and coughed. He tried to swallow. The girl smiled at him patiently.

He didn't know why he felt so odd, so scared. He thought if he opened his mouth he would…pass…out. Pass into…hell. He had to leave.

"I'm sorry, Miss. I…."

A loud, constant honking saved him, brought him head-rattlingly back to real time.

He turned to watch a battered Ford pickup truck whip into the parking lot, its brakes squealing, dust swirling behind it. A high school boy in knee-ripped jeans and a grease-stained white t-shirt jumped from the cab, slamming the door shut with a cat-like flick of his wrist. The boy flashed to the clerk's window. Jack instinctively stepped back and away from the boy, a blond, crew-cut All-American dervish. This boy needed room to dance.

Then Jack noticed the pearl handle of a pistol sticking out of the waistband at the boy's belly.

Jack backed up a couple more steps.

Lots of room to dance.

The boy stood at the clerk's window, trembling, gazing wide-eyed enraged into the girl's blank face. His fists clenched tightly at his sides twice, three times, four. Jack thought of a crazed gunfighter in some hyperbolic, blood-spurting movie.

He'd always thought the fluttering pulsation mere symbolism. Pumping blood out. Letting rage in. Rage hated life. Blood was life.

He studied the boy's hands. White-knuckled angry.

No life. No time.

Had there been any time spent between the boy slamming the truck's door and his hyperventilating at the clerk's window? Had rage opened a door in time? Was that why you were always just a second late or a second early when you tried to stop some act of horror?

And then the boy's hands relaxed, became soft, almost old looking.

Jack got scared then. Really scared.

"It's true," the boy whispered, his face bloodless and contorted, sweat glistening on his smooth high forehead. Jack imagined him as maybe five years old, on the verge of tears, searching for words he hadn't mastered. A death's head boy with a gun for a belly. Angry and beyond the confines of time.

"The bastard left for California," he blurted out, his head jerking forward and back like he was tapping out the words in the air, sending secret code. His breathing quickened as he spoke. Working the rage back into his soul blood, he clenched his fists convulsively. And then those flashing, timeless hands shot out and he threw his white straw cowboy hat to the ground, kicked it, and kicked it again. It tumbled away into the parking lot, got caught in a dust devil, crossed the highway, and disappeared.

"The bastard, the bastard!" he hissed, his cast-down eyes darting across the cracked black lot. Jack caught an image. The boy was searching for an invisible snake hiding in the dust trails, one waiting to strike at him, to devour him. A tightness gripped the boy's temples. Jack wondered what it meant.

Either he wanted to be swallowed up in the jaws of a bigger fear or he was desperate for something, anything to stomp on. Something needed smashing. He had to smash back into real time or be caught in a timeless nightmare.

Jack remembered that feeling. He remembered when he needed to smash into the earth, smash with the force of dynamite, blow a hole into the underworld with his stomping-pure fear and frightful rage, stomp straight down to hell and feed the devil himself from the gaping, wounded pit of his confused and broken soul. It wasn't that long ago. Not that long ago at all.

Jack looked at the gun again, took another step back, and searched for an exit. Across the highway he spotted a white cinder block café roasting shadeless and alone in the afternoon heat. An ancient phone booth leaned against it like the last drunk suitor from a long forgotten dance. The black tinted windows glared unmoved at the passing world. Jack couldn't tell if anyone were in there or not. But welcoming it wasn't. He audibly sighed, then worriedly covered his mouth with a tight fist.

No sanctuary.

The girl stared mutely past the boy, passive, disengaged—from her seat in another world she watched some distant bird tumbling dead through a water soft sky.

Her reddish complexion changed when the boy said California; the weary face opened, became shining, serene, surrendered.

"That'll be $54 with tax. Room 2," she cooed, pushing the key toward Jack. The flat, false tone startled him. It sounded utterly disconnected from the boy's passion, from the obvious seriousness of the situation.

Things were falling apart. This was how it began: a slippage, a warp. First the boy, now the girl.

"Not again," he found himself saying out loud as he mechanically opened his wallet.

The girl's brow furrowed and she pulled the old brass key back.

"No," she said. Her voice deepened, aging 40 years in a breath. "Room 9. Check out is noon, but it's always noon somewhere. We got no room service. Star has decent food though. Enjoy your stay."

She placed the new key in Jack's hand, plucked the three twenties he held out to her, and pushed them into her bosom, all in one slow, dream-honey slow, movement.

The boy never looked at Jack. They weren't really in the same dimension. The boy's gaze followed the girl as she rose and slowly, regally, floated out the office door. She stopped for a moment at the entrance of Room 1, the room she had been in when Jack first saw her, then moved on to Room 2, unlocked the door and walked in, closing the door behind her without turning around.

Jack and the boy waited silently in the shadow of the building, suspended in their separate dimensions. Neither of them seemed to have the ability to move. The air lost its oxygen, the light paled, the earth sagged. Jack felt his muscles loosen from the bone. His hands curled in on themselves.

Falling apart. Memory spiraling into the future. He saw her on the beach, a vision muted through tears or ocean spray. Is it time that keeps everything from happening at once or is it something in the eye, in the heart?

Falling apart again in a slow dissolve.

The boy suddenly turned and walked up to Jack. Jack raised his hand impulsively to the boy's shoulder.

"It'll be okay," Jack said tenderly, his hand suspended above the boy's shoulder, feeling the rage held there, held in both of them, a rage born in helplessness. "Just give her time," Jack said slowly, withdrawing his hand to rest over his own pounding heart. "Go in there and just sit with her. Just sit with her and be there. Be there."

The boy studied Jack's face, looking for something, some point to smash. But as he entered Jack's eyes they became a hidden, magical place that he might crawl into, a slip in time and space, a place of sanctuary for himself and his friend.

"Okay," the boy finally said. "She needs me, doesn't she?"

"Yes," Jack whispered. "You need each other. Everyone needs someone. It's our nature. We need each other. And right now that is what you two need to know. So, you go on in. Need. Be needed. But, uh, could you…give me the gun?"

The boy nodded as Jack spoke. Nodded as in a dream time trance, but he kept the gun. He turned and walked stiffly back to his truck, eased the gun from his waistband, and put it in the glove compartment. Without a further look at Jack, he then walked to the girl's door. He knocked once. Jack didn't hear an answer, but the boy pushed the door open and disappeared into the darkness of the room, his pale face a bleak moon as he turned and closed the door behind him.

Jack had been tired, had wanted only to sleep when he had walked to the clerk's window. Now, the thought of sleeping terrified him. He remembered that when things were falling apart he had to be vigilant. Or was it the opposite?

He pocketed the key and decided to try the café.

A strong smell of coffee and cleaning fluid hit him when he pushed open the door. Coffee, Lysol, and very cold air. Only the heat at his back kept him from turning around.

The place was empty, but smoke from a burning cigarette curled from an ashtray at the far end of the counter. A bell rang when he opened the door and a waitress stepped around from behind the coffee machine to his left. She wore a pink uniform with a pink ceramic pig pinned to her ample bosom. Her sugar white hair stood like a steel sculpture of cotton candy atop her small, deer shaped head. Jack smiled instantly as she raised a tiny hand and gestured as if daintily sipping coffee.

"Yes, thank you," he chuckled as his eyes adjusted to the bright pinkness of the interior. Paintings of pigs hung on the walls which were themselves wallpapered with scenes of a pig farm rendered in kindergarten book style. A black velvet pig a la Elvis hung just behind the cash register. A hand-painted TCB in gold script arched over it. Just under the Elvis was a blackboard with a chalked message that read: If a heart ain't broken, it can never be healed.

That one stopped Jack cold. It was too close, too something. But then the waitress entered from the back with a huge coffee cup shaped like a 1930's Porky. He couldn't help but laugh.

"This ought to do you, honey," she chirped. "Hot, fresh, and plenty. And watch that mind of yours, hon'. It'll get you in trouble. Hi, my name's Petunia. What's yours?"

She stuck out her small hand straight and stiff as a tin soldier.

"J…Jack," Jack said, almost forgetting his new name. "It's nice to meet you, Petunia. I, uh, love your place."

"Oh, this isn't mine. I just work here. Well, if you call it working. It belongs to Virgil Denton. You'll meet him directly, but pay him no mind. Specially once he starts telling his stories. You're a good man. So you just listen to The Virgil. Don't answer no questions. Keep your mouth shut on the important stuff, right? He'll just gobble you up. Now, whachu wanna eat, honey?"

"You know, Petunia, I'm not really that hungry."

"Oh, honey, you gotta eat. Hmm? Pork chops. That's the thing for a boy like you. Pork chops, gravy, and mashed potatoes. It'll look good on ya."

"Well...," Jack hedged.

"Honey, first thing you gotta know about me is there ain't no winning against me, so you just drink that coffee and think about the top button on them jeans and how good it's gonna feel popping it."

"Okay, Petunia. Pork chops, it is."

"You're gone make some lucky lady one fine husband, Jack."

"I don't know."

"What'd I say about argying with me, honey? You just believe in ol' Petunia and don't you fret."

"Yes, ma'am."

"That's better. Lookit here. The Virgil. Perfect timing. He'll chat ya up while I fix them chops. And remember what I said about not paying him no mind. Just listen and nod politely."

Jack watched Petunia disappear into the recesses of the kitchen and, infected by Petunia's exuberance, turned on his bar stool anticipating the arrival of The Virgil. But the pig pink door didn't open and no shadows crossed the windows. Puzzled, Jack swung back around. At the far end of the counter an old man hunched over an ashtray staring into the blue smoke rising from the nearly burnt out cigarette. He sucked in a deep lungful of the stink and sneered at Jack.

He was as corpse-eating ugly as Petunia was elfin. His right arm curled, twisted and shriveled against his chest. The hand, a shadow-fist goose-head tapping spastically at his heart.

"The ghosts got the word," The Virgil squeaked, his voice like a crack-pated squirrel. The sneer stayed as the old man spoke, plastered there, Jack presumed, due to the same condition that crippled his arm.

"Come on down here," The Virgil commanded. "Can't see your eyes. Gotta see a man's eyes. Why I don't use the telephone. Lies too easy on the telephone. Easy enough as it is. Women love telephones. Come on, partner, move on down. Ain't that hard a work even for you."

Jack's shoulders dropped. The muscles loosening again. Falling apart. The Virgil was the parts man, the junk dealer, the renderer of souls. Jack floated to the end of the bar. Everything slow, dizzying, compelling. He had never believed in free will. You were either lucky or unlucky. Either you had the gods with you or you didn't. If you pulled yourself out of a scrape it was only because you had been given the ability to pull yourself out of the scrape at birth or in that particular, grace-filled moment. Self-will was an illusion as you were pulled apart by the varying gods who fought constantly for the possession of your soul.

Now some mad god possessed him and the others, the ones who were kinder masters, had fallen asleep. There was nothing he could do but watch as his life energy streamed into the sinkhole of The Virgil's cynicism.

"At the Suicide Motel, aren't you?" The Virgil continued, pulling a sucking drag from the exhausted cigarette. His mouth could only open on the left side, making for a two finger-sized hole that kept him alive. His nose was flattened, the nostrils little more than dimples, useless for breathing.

"What's your room number? Never mind. We'll know soon enough. So what's your story? Woman? Probably a woman. Most are. Let me tell you about women. Wanna know? Hell, no, you don't. People don't want to really know. They only want fairy tales. Not the truth. Lies feel good. Let the tigers eat your soul but you don't feel a thing. People are stupid. Men especially. Women's what does it. Telling the lies about love. Now, now. You're thinkin' I'm just a burnt out old fart. Bumpkin in the West. Redneck.

"Don't know nothing about beauty cause I'm ugly. Truth, real truth, don't come dressed up in a sweet Jesus face all soft and gooey and smelling like mother's milk. People are so predictable."

Jack pointed at the Aquafina bottle next to the ashtray.

"Sure, have at it, partner. Truth's always hard to swallow."

Jack straightened, a shot of courage inexplicably coursing through his chest. He wiped the mouth of the bottle.

Virgil leaned back and looked down his nonexistent nose. "I ain't communicable? You?"

Jack ignored him and wiped the rim one more time. He took a big slug and immediately and uncontrollably sprayed the contents into The Virgil's face. Jack tried to sputter out a protest between hacks, but Virgil had to speak for him.

"That's right, it's vodka. Hell, I don't drink nothing else, partner," The Virgil sniffed, stiffly shaking his head and wiping his face with his red-checked gingham sleeve.

"Buh…buh," Jack mumbled tapping at the bottle label and briskly shaking his head.

"What? You one of those fellers who believe everything you read?"

Jack chuckled, wiping his mouth with the back of a hand. "Hey, you got me, Virgil. You're a…funny man. Is there some of the non-alcohol version of that stuff around?"

The fear left him. The other gods were awake and contending again.

"So what's your story?" The Virgil asked again, ignoring Jack's request.

"Well, you got me all around, Virg. Women and fairy tales. That pretty much pegs me."

"Figures. I thought you were thirsty?" He nodded behind Jack. Jack turned to his left and there was a bottle of Aquafina, sweating cold.

***

"So," The Virgil said, his voice suddenly deep and strong, "there was this prince, handsome, brave, noble. Like you, like me, like every man when you take the fear away. He was in love. Lucky man, for the woman he loved loved him back. But something happened. Always does. Has to. A test. Always a test.

"His lover was kidnapped. Taken by a witch. Possessed, some psychologist told me. But they have their own stories and this one's mine. The witch took her not to punish the girl or the prince, but to punish the girl's father—a man who, when he was tested, had failed, had lied. Now, the psychologists can do with that what ever they like and I might even agree with them. Except, we're all daddies, and we all fail some time or another. So what matters is that this guy's failure cost someone else, and he still wouldn't face the music. People always willing to put someone else in the fire, blame them for their troubles. Ain't many who know to get in the fire themselves if they want to be free. But, hell, I gave up preaching. Anyway, the boy, the prince, went after his girl.

"He traveled deep into the forest and he met an old, tired man sitting in the knot hole of a big ol' fig tree. The old man stuck out a shriveled old miserable arm and asked for a piece of bread, any ol' piece of bread: moldy, wet, even, white. He didn't care.

"The prince wasn't one of them pucker butted yahoos who thinks he's… what?…'Enabling poverty with the poor exercise of charity,' so he pulls a loaf from his saddlebag and hands it on over to the old codger.

"The old man smack wolves about half that sucker down in no time, then mumbles something about being sure not to kill anything in that there wood, and if he managed that, then the prince would be sure to get his girl back. The prince is fine with that. Sure, the Daddy would probably want the witch burning in hell before the whistle blew, but the boy didn't much want to kill anyone. He just wanted the girl. The girl and a peaceful life. Comfort, you know? That's all any of us want. To be at home. Comfortable in our own skins with our loved ones being the same. It's really not much to ask, you'd think. Yeah. Well, you'd be wrong.

"So, the prince, he rode on into the forest and pretty soon he came to a waterfall. Beautiful. Mists like dancing diamonds. Rainbows one on top of the other just walking up to heaven. Blue, blue heaven. Ice blue vodka heaven. Such a sharp, tasty blue. And the music of those waters. Stop your heart. Too beautiful, really.

"And there, sitting on a rock peppered with peacocks and doves, there in the middle of the pool at the bottom of the waterfall sat the princess, so tiny, so afraid, so very much alone. In all that gorgeousness it was like she was surrounded by the blackest of blacks with only slivers of the palest light barely grazing her cheekbones, the tip of her slender nose. Her beautiful eyes mere specks dimming, dimming. There was nothing else to her. It was like she was floating on a dark sea. Floating, but sinking slowly, sinking because she had waited so long and the heaviness of the waiting was killing her, pulling her down, and any moment, that very moment, she would finally slip all the way under, be swallowed by that dark water and be gone forever.

"The prince jumped from his horse and cried out her name. Cried it loud and long, running. Running. Running straight into her heart. And she rose. She rose up and her face, her face was like a rose unfolding in the morning sun. The dew on her cheeks reflecting the brilliance of a thousand morning suns. He had come. He would not let her go.

"But the witch, the witch rose up, too. She rose up like a tiger out of the tall cutting grass of the jungle. She was a tiger. A tiger running right at the princess from the darkness of the cave behind the waterfall. The princess could not see it because she only had eyes for the prince. But he could see. Could see his life dripping from the mouth of a heartless beast. He raised his pistol and aimed. But he couldn't pull the trigger. The old man's voice saying, 'Shoot above the beast's head. Scare it. Scare it good.' And he pulled up and fired, once, twice, three, four.

"But as he shot a dove flew up frightened by the tiger and it fell dead, shot through the heart. Snap. The girl vanished, turned to a watery mist. And the tiger stood on its hind legs. Swoosh. The witch. She looked at the prince so sadly and then she laughed. Laughed and laughed.

"Sad, ain't it? Try to do the right thing. Listen to people, and there's your life, blasted, falling bloody feathers in a cloudy mist.

"But, hey, he had tried to do the right thing. The witch had no choice but to give him a second chance. Law of the universe, right? Second chances for every fool. So the prince finds himself at the back of the waterfall. The witch standing on a ledge high above him. Too far to shoot her which is what he wanted to do. Hell, if he was gonna kill something and lose it all anyway, why not the witch, you know? He was confused, afraid. Ashamed. Hard place to be. But eventually we all stand there looking up and wondering who to trust. Can't trust those outsiders, but can you trust yourself? All those mistakes you've made? Last person to trust is yourself, eh?

"Three passages open before him. Through one of them the princess waits. But the other two hold tigers. Choose the right one and he could have what he desired. Choose wrong and he's…well, second chances are like first ones: they have conditions.

"Each passage the same. Black and rocky and filled with the cries of his lover. Right? Left? The path just in front of his nose? What logic can you follow? Head, heart, or soul? Ah, a three card monte set up by a witch. Fear of making the wrong choice. Fear of not making a choice at all. Maybe he could sit for a while, draw the witch down and put a gun to her head. Maybe he could go down any path and if there's a tiger he'd just shoot it.

"But what if the witch had dressed his love in a tiger skin? What to do? What does a prince possess that we don't? Can a prince decide where a mere mortal falters? What would you do?

***

"So what's your room number?"

Jack stared at the old man, enraptured by the tale. It took him a few seconds to realize The Virgil had finished the story.

"Did you know," the old man continued, "that every room in that motel has held a suicide? Every room but one."

Jack shook his head no.

"Yeah," The Virgil smiled. "So, what's the room number, partner?"

Jack opened his mouth to say, but remained silent. He took a slug from his Aquafina.

"Figures. Petunia likes ya, don't she?"

Jack shrugged his shoulders, nervously popped the squirt top of the plastic water bottle up and down, up and down. Still, he kept eye contact with The Virgil. Something in him couldn't help but look into Virgil's eyes. Something that recognized a man who had lived a lifetime falling apart.

"Hell, it don't matter," The Virgil laughed in a short, mangled roar. "They're all tigers. Your number'll come up one day, partner. Always does. Always does."

The Virgil whirled on his seat and hopped down to the floor. He was tiny, maybe four and a half feet tall. He limped into a back room without another word.

"And, you know something else, honey? There are also ladies down every one of them damn paths." It was Petunia. She slid a steaming plate of pork chops, mashed potatoes, and gravy in front of Jack as if she'd been waiting for her cue.

"But The Virgil wouldn't see that," the magical waitress continued. "He's too certain of what he knows. Too bitter. Has no sense of humor. Thinks life's all cruel and sentimental. Poor Virgil. Don't listen to him, honey. It'll take the joy out of you. I'd rather wrestle with those tigers than live in terror of them. Poor ol' Virgil. Another cup?"

Jack smiled vaguely at the magical woman, her sugary hair like a beacon in his falling apart life.

"Sure, Petunia. I'll have another cup."

"You sure? Maybe you oughta get some sleep," she said with a wink.

"Maybe you're right, ma'am."

"Like I said, honey: You believe in ol' Petunia. And you're lucky. The Virgil liked you. I can tell. So, you just get on to bed and you get back to that tower, okay?"

She had him out the door and halfway across the highway before he realized she had spoken of the tower. And then she was gone, the lights out in the café, and he was waking up to the sound of a honking truck.

His car was ready. The mechanics had towed it back to him. Seemed there was a pump at the garage after all.

Jack walked as in a dream to the check out window. A middle aged Hispanic man sat in the clerk's seat.

"Hi," Jack said. "Here's the key. Room 9. Uh, where's the girl?"

"What girl?"

"The pregnant girl."

"Don't know what you're talking about, mister," the man said sourly, then reached up and abruptly pulled down a shade that read CLOSED.

Jack looked at the door to Room 2. He took a step toward it, then stopped. He shrugged and walked across the highway. The door to the café was locked. Jack pressed his face to a window. The place was empty. But on the blackboard behind the cash register two messages were scrawled in pink chalk.

One read: Second chances are choices of the heart.

The other read: There are no answers, partner. Only stories.

Jack looked at his reflection in the glass of the restaurant, opened his mouth and held it open for a few seconds. He studied his eyes, the lines in his forehead. Opened his mouth again and said, "Broken? Open? What do you do?"

He leaned back and looked down the highway. A dust devil swirled silently along a distant ridge. Beyond it, darkness and a promise of rain.

Jack had found his passage home.

The Tower

The lead of the story in his head read: *This achievement marks a milestone in history akin to walking on the moon or curing cancer. It will change society, validate the arc of history, and redeem the bitter tears shed by countless fire-veined revolutionaries and tormented, ashen-faced poets.*

The curse is ended. It is done. The problem of language solved. And the simplicity of it goes without saying, all such things being elegant. True elegance, simplicity itself. As is vexation and the source of the rebels' shaking fists and the poets' poignant tears.

For there has always been but one reason to curse the ways of the world. But one. And here it is: Faith and love are real; humanity is good, decent, and worth preserving; needing other people is a sign of strength; dreams and reality are interdependent; our lives and all lives matter.

So, okay, maybe there is more than one reason. Life is too grand to be reduced. But if it were reducible, that magic, breakthrough knowledge in a nutshell has to be love. Love lying curled, tongue to toe, at the still, wide-eyed-pupil center of the mystery of mysteries, the slippery I yam what I yam that defies the grasp of any sense. Love infinitely spreading, arms thrown wide to hold an impossibly pregnant void, leaning over the abyss at the furthest edges of the universe, there where time's first stars still thinly yearn to swoon into their own involuted immanence.

There we always are, blindly drunk though we be on our own thin, beliefs. Hold me up, sailor. I've seen your face in the stars.

"What is it like to never let go? What is it like for God?"

Winding back, even into history, love turns even in the breathless red eye of the cruelest act of violence.

"A love betrayed or denied?" she asks.

He smiles, "Yes, most certainly, yes. It is there in the blank eye of that most wrenching maelstrom."

"Still, still. Be still, Jack," she soothes. "And must you be so Biblical?"

He turns half around and his voice quietens, but does not cease.

"Love is there, stirring our yearnings. Your yearning, yes, for recognition. To be known. To be re-known. It knows and has known. It sees through even that reflecting blackness that frightens us to our core in our most wrenching of nightmares. Though demons dance on the empty surface, it is love's eye, and it always sees the essential value of human life, of its need to cherish and be cherished. Who could deny that? Truthfully deny that? The surface of the moon, the rupturing of time and space: these dreams of historic conquest are but corollaries to the quest for the heart, the holy grail of yearning that is you and me and all that is in between."

"She who claims the unknown makes history, Jack. But who are you selling?"

He quietly closes the newspaper in his mind and looks out at the passing desert.

The Virgil's Truth: there are no right answers, no wrong answers—only your answers, your story, a story within a story.

Jack had seen the unknown, had wrestled with a demon and been brought to his knees. Brought to his knees and he surrendered, fell into an acceptance greater than any victory he had ever imagined in his hard push toward wisdom. How easy it seemed now. How foolish his resistance, his ego and intellectualism. But he even laughed at this fool-found wisdom. All necessary. All valuable. All his story. It wasn't resistance or ego or intellectualism or cowardice or even bravery that blocked him, that kept him stuck. It was his resistance, his ego until it wasn't. The walls were an illusion. A necessary illusion. Illusions were divine, too.

Jack was enthralled. He was sold on everything.

He laughed all the way back to California. Laughed and dreamed up headlines, songs, philosophical blurbs, and glib ad copy. The Virgil's Truth. He loved it.

And the best part, he told himself, was that he wouldn't publish any of it. No telling someone how to live their life. Their life was a story, a love story. What more could he say? How could he sell a soul a book for a saw buck. A book with four sentences:

Life is a love story, your unique love story. All second chances are choices of the heart. There are only stories, stories within stories within stories without end.

And the coup de grace: There are no definitive answers, partner.

Every few miles he pulled his Jeep to the side of the road and just sat and stared out into the desert grinning. Wellness looked nothing like he had imagined.

"No preconceived notions. Just step up and keep walking into the face of the beast."

Talking to himself. Waving his arms. Shaking his head.

"A loon for a guide. A loon on the broken carousel. Sing it, Daft One, sing it. 'Baaahhhhh dada da da da da ta. Ba dada da da da da ta. Ba dada da ta. Ba dada da ta. Ba dada da da da da ta. Hoo Hoo.'"

Occasionally his new found energy drew him from the cab of his Jeep and out into the brush. Felt like the gloved hands of God Almighty grabbed him by the lapels and flung him over the mountains. He landed with a solid thud and leapt like a Mary Martin Peter Pan over the wire fences that lined the rights of way of the interstate. He waved wildly, joyously at passing motorists who honked at him, sometimes with a frown but mostly they just grinned at the fool.

Fools, they have their allies.

"You know, sometimes, you can't dance when you want to. You have to hold everything in. Measure out joy like it's iridium from Mars. Precious, precious. At best, just let the tip of it show or else thieves will come, demons or the grey ones. Or measure it out like it's a poison. Take too much joy into the ol' soul and you'll die they say. Keel right over. Rise in your mortal coils like Methuselah, too good for this covetous old world.

"So best to be careful with the public displays of wild, childlike abandon. Be discreet or they'll come and take it all away. Take you away, by god, for acting the mooncalf!

"This place is a vale of tears, not a wonder. Everyone knows that. So, how dare you take a moment and dance off into the desert on a Tuesday afternoon? Joy is to be measured out—like it's a poison. Use just enough, just a pinch each day, only a tad a week, a dollop a month, and one day—say the day you die—you'll be utterly immune to joy and all that you missed out on."

So Jack ran, leapt, skipped, danced further into the desert.

He'd bought a notebook at his last gas station stop. His regular journal lay on his night stand. This hadn't been a planned trip. Who knew there'd be so much to tell, so much that might evaporate in the rush of joy's muchness. He had to write it down, write it down fast.

A mile or two into the desert he climbed up into the shadows of an outcropping of tumble rock.

"Maybe there'll be rattlers to pet," he grinned. But he didn't find any. He climbed to the very top of the grey mound of boulders and did a little tap dance.

"In school they don't teach you the things you'll most treasure. She worried more about numbers, counting by twos, and opening the right end of the milk carton at lunch. Like you wouldn't figure out that stuff on your own. Like that stuff mattered."

He pulled the notebook from his hip pocket and wrote:

Illusion is the first of all pleasure—Voltaire.
Perpetual pleasure is no pleasure—Wisdom of the Folk.
Do It As Yer Duty and Yer All Done For—Jack.
Burden lifted. Countdown to freedom. One, two, skip a few, 99, a hundred.

Kids. How he loved the kid inside him, the kid The Virgil had somehow set loose upon the world. Jack was freed now from trembling in corners real and imaginary, of spending years and years being pursued by a monster that no longer existed, hadn't existed for years.

So many people dominated by phantasms. Their childhood years gone, the torturers dead or weakened, powerless in a reality divorced from the past. How many lived in dread of the tyrants of that past, tyrants still ruling the images crawling through an endless, lightless maze in the soul of that adult swaddled tightly by fantasies of utter helplessness?

We all have our monsters. We all have the kid. Fantasies. Which would you choose? So choose. It's an empirical choice. It makes your reality.

He wrote furiously. No one could possibly read his scrawl.

All humans experience these issues of the soul, but in every human the issues vary, just enough so we are unique in the universe—or universes. It's more than just timing or gender, race, or age. There is that thing, that marvelous, unknowable, you-can't-catch-me stinker of a yi-ti-yo thing. It rolls around in each of us.

"I bow to your objection, Jill, before you even voice it," he said to a mottled beetle crawling across his knee. Then he scribbled again in his notebook.

The monster rolls around, too. So, I will entertain it thusly:

Yet in those differences, suffering hides. It hides and seeks an answer to the monsters who suck joy from our life with twisted pictures from a past...a real past that caused real pain, pain that exists now only in shadows. The monster exists only in shadows. You freely give that monster energy. Give it to the monster or free the child. Choose!

If we look past those vampiric monsters of the past to a wonder that was there before the monsters existed.... If we can open enough, or close enough, for that matter, we can bring to ourselves, bring to the world, our story of beauty—our own story of that...that thing between the monster and the child—the us that is more than feelings, more than thoughts, that thing that is.... That thing that is me and that I can't speak to in any way other than story. A story that, because it is mine, is absolutely unique—unique and therefore unrepeatable.

"Unrepeatable?" he said aloud, voicing Jill's imaginary rejoinder. "Then, is that a valid measure? Testing and getting the same results, isn't that how things are proved?"

O, yes. But we claim new images. We are valid. Our now is valid. Our strength and beauty unfolding is as valid as the sapping past. Our soul knowledge calls beyond the realm of science...or history.

"Look to the smile on your face!"

Look to the smile!

Throughout the day Jack wrote in small, intense bursts, imagining that the woman in the tower sat beside him arguing, cajoling, testing his new found sense of self. But then his awareness would stretch beyond the page and he left off writing to follow the sound of a distant bird or the swirling of a wind or the curving of a light on a distant sage bush: he followed messages of mystery that couldn't be pinned down in a word.

An hour or two would pass in his meanderings before he circled back to his Jeep and continued on his journey watching the desert pass by in silence. Feeling an intense desire to hear a human voice, he turned on the radio and listened to whatever he could tune in. And he listened intently. Each song, each conversation a story. Even the formula songs, the tritest of popular talk hosts, the crassest taste caressed him with its need for acceptance.

Smiling indulgently, he remembered how dismissive he had been of a woman who once told him she just wanted to belong. Such a desire for inclusion certainly had been and was the catalyst for unspeakable acts as well as acts of mere mediocrity. But even as he heaped hip scorn unto the young woman, he realized his own need, his own desire to matter, to be included in the universe's fold. The exclusionary act of mattering, though different, was still the reach of belonging, a mattering no less aching in its need.

Homecoming queens or social critics, each longed to be unique in a field of equals. To be welcomed. To be at home.

Jill's voice wrestled with him continuously in these meditations. Always now she took his cynical voice, the one he knew so well from young adulthood onward. It had weakened when he first met her. Nearly gone these last few weeks. It teased him with her honeyed tone.

"But do we not need 'Not Home,'" she asked? "A place where adventure happens, the realm of Hermes beyond the border, where writing happens and art and where that *thing* is maybe even more at home?"

Yes, yes. Don't get me wrong. I'm not an absolutist. I know the need for the strange, the dangerous, the inexplicable, the need for the disastrous. I know the fool's price for not respecting the gift's of the shadow. You taught me that. Still, I say, lean to the joy. The argument goes on and on and convincing never gets enough.

She eased back into the shadows of his consciousness and he drove on through the late afternoon and into the night. He stopped several times to walk out into the desert evening. Blue skies spread wide and soft, the sunset plum and violet with the bright full moon rising over a mesa like a crystal ball of good fortune and peaceful times.

Going home. Loved, protected, cherished.

About midnight Jack turned off the main highway and drove a mile into nowhere. He eased onto the shoulder and stopped. Dragging a blanket from under the seat, he walked about ten yards into the dark, spread the blanket without a word, and curled gently into its folds. He slept soundly under the stars, woke at dawn, and drove the last 200 miles without stopping once to write. He rode in silence. But the smile never left his face.

Arriving north of the tower just before noon, he cut the engine on the rise above the beach, and sat in the cab for a few minutes staring across the water and breathing slowly, deeply, wanting to be...ready. Ready for anything.

He stepped onto the caliche road. A strong, cooling wind blew in from the grey green ocean.

Winds all the way from China, he mused.

A couple of surfers bobbed in the chop waiting for a curl. The gift of a courteous Japanese bow, Jack laughed to himself. Blessed by gods from afar.

Further to the west, raucous gulls circled the stern of a scow returning from the Channel Islands. The islands were ghosts today. Ashen waves against a white sky.

Clarity. What he had wanted more than anything these last few months was clarity. He turned from the sea to gaze down onto the tower. It was visible, visible in full daylight. He hadn't known if that was possible. If this was madness, he was full in it and so be it. This place was clearly his home.

The gulls called closer. A few glided above him. He shaded his eyes against the high sun to see their dark silhouettes. What gulls had he brought back from his journey? What beggary floated in his soul? Who was he trying to sell? None and no one he hoped. The next time he saw her he would be needful of…nothing. But he would be thankful for the time he might spend with her.

Jack drove to his old house and packed a few things. He showered, shaved, and called a real estate agent and his attorney. All the arrangements were made in an amazingly short time. By dusk he sat on the eastern ridge overlooking the tower.

It was time. He was ready.

He stepped onto the porch, closed his eyes and said a quick Hail Mary. He smiled and turned the glass knob. The door was locked. Locked. He took at few steps back and looked up. At the ceiling of the porch. He knew he wasn't back far enough to see windows. He was disoriented, embarrassed.

"Stupid," he said aloud to himself. All the confidence hard gained in the last two days vanished in an instant. Gone, trailing clouds of thieving gulls.

"Close your eyes. Breathe. Life is good, yes? Even when it whips us about like we were so much flotsam in a cyclone." It was her voice. He walked back toward the door and tried again. Still locked. He suddenly felt like a stalker, a man with no manners, some lug looking for an excuse to force entry into a place he wasn't welcomed.

His head tracked left and right, up and down in short jerks as if he were robotically searching for an invisible fly. His heart shriveled knowing it was self-pity mewling this pathetic ruse, a ruse meant for some nonexistent judge watching him from a safe distance, declaring him a gull. Still, he backed slowly away from the door and off the porch, stumbling backwards on the two steps and then shamefully looking again towards the sea as he hurried to his Jeep fumbling with his keys. And then they fell into a mud hole and he stopped.

"It's okay," he said to himself. "You're afraid. You always go back to the defenses you learned as a child when you're afraid. Stoop. Retrieve the keys. Turn around. Look at the cliffs. There is no one there. No one to judge you. No one who can judge you. You…I am comparable to no one now. It's just me and the mystery. I judge myself. That's harsh enough. I'm judging myself. Harshly. I'm not going to blame…. Defy the judge. Bring out the fool."

He covered his face with his hands and loudly blubber-brrred through his slack loose lips. "Ohhh-kaaay!" He sh-sh-shook the word out bodily into the universe with a giddy, goofy, accepting exasperation. "My heart is a revving engine! Where do we gah-gah goh?" Hands outstretched he turned slowly around and around stopping on the third complete turn to bow at each of the eight directions

Calm washed back into his body. "There. We've all had our say. Lots of time," he thought. "Lots of time to make more mistakes. Lots of time to forgive. And the headline reads: Slow Down. There's Plenty of Time in Infinity. You're not crazy. Sane just doesn't look like it used to."

Headlights bounced along the ground around him. He turned to face them, smiling serenely. It might be her he thought, but if not…. He was ready for anything.

A dark Jaguar sedan pulled to a stop just to the front and slightly left of Jack. The lights stayed on and the windows were tinted so there was no seeing into the car. He shaded his eyes and tightly smiled as he bent to gesture a hello.

The engine raced a couple of times then cut off, sputtering a few times before backfiring and dying.

"Jaguars," he muttered under his breath.

Curse words rang through the air as the driver's side door popped open and then swung back to catch the driver in the knee. More curse words followed as a woman in a long dark dress stepped from the car.

She clutched a briefcase in one hand and fumbled with a knot of keys in the other. The car alarm went off. Jack hurried over to help. He got the briefcase from her.

"Thanks," she said, a sparkling smile rising and just as quickly disappearing across her pale face in a mercurial false flash before she promptly and grimly turned her attention back to the knot of keys. She aimed frantically at the car, pressing first one and then another black plastic tab until the annoying blaring and blinking finally ceased.

He studied her back. Shoulder blades of a fairy, he thought. But she probably doesn't know.

She turned around suddenly as if just remembering Jack was behind her. "Hi," she said, far too loudly, then turned, clicked one time over her shoulder and the headlights came back on but without the noise. "My name is Amanda. Amanda Pace. I'm with Guy Realty. I'm so sorry I'm late. You know they tell you you'll make a million dollars in real estate but they don't tell you it'll cost you a million and a half in therapy for all the crap you have to go through. No days off, never home, always late. Constant state of distrust. No, you don't need to hear that, do you? Of course not. Hi. Thanks. Amanda. Amanda Pace. Say it twice because people don't listen. Not their fault. It's just that people don't listen. They're always looking for the loophole. The deal. The way out. Everybody's a ticket. So I understand you want this place like yesterday and I know I'm late. The traffic from L.A. is...well, you know the five. God, I hate it. So anyway...God, I am a mess. I'm so sorry. Lucky for you I am a very good realtor when it comes to terms. I know you'll be very happy here. I love it already."

Jack raised his hand to his lips and made a shushing gesture. To no avail. She was incredibly beautiful. He gazed into her face amazed. He felt himself floating in a strange calming light that surrounded her face and reached out to surround him and caress him in a gentle warmth recalled from a time he wasn't even sure he remembered as real. But he knew it as intimately as he knew his own breathing. The wall of words couldn't disguise her reach.

Jack hadn't listened to a word from the moment she said her name until she mentioned that she loved the tower.

He reached out and put two fingers on her lips. She stopped talking, but she didn't pull back even as Jack let his fingers linger there, pressing gently, then stroking down, pulling the lower lip open and then releasing it, rubbing his fingers as if feeling silk as he brought them back to his own lips.

"Ms. Pace," he said softly. "You are much too beautiful to have to apologize to strangers for being late. At least to this stranger. Your competence is, no doubt, as great as your ability to negotiate the five. I don't even try. So, could you just tell me what you and I are doing here? Or rather who you think I am."

"Well, you're the man I'm supposed to meet here. She said you'd be here and here you are. She didn't say you were a charmer, but that's okay. I wouldn't have believed her anyway. I've had enough of charmers. I…I think I…excuse me."

She turned away and Jack realized she was crying. He wanted to stroke her hair. He wanted to hold her face up to his and kiss away the tears slowly, gently, tracing them to her soft red lips.

He cleared his throat and pushed a blue bandana over her right shoulder.

She looked back at him. Her eyes wet, two lines of mascara-laced tears curving over her pale cheeks. Her lips parted as if to speak. She took a step toward him. The moon peered from behind a cloud. She stopped and looked, for the first time, directly into his eyes.

Jack thought of a tree covered in white blossoms standing alone on the top of a bare ridge. A ray of sun over a distant mountain range strikes the tree making the blossoms sparkle like diamonds against the blackness of the range. It holds for a glorious moment looking as if it were the tree of life, the tree of knowledge, the most sacred and magical of trees to have ever lived, and then the sun goes down and the tree becomes a muddied grey, slumping into oblivion.

"I'm sorry," Amanda said taking the kerchief and dabbing delicately at her eyes. "It's no concern of yours."

"No, Ms. Pace, I have never felt more concerned in all my life."

"What a sweet thing to say. But I'm being very unprofessional."

"What? You're being human?"

"Yes, heaven forbid, eh? Listen. I need you to sign this." She turned and laid her briefcase on the hood of her car, popped the locks and drew out a ribboned bundle of papers.

"She insisted, I was told," Amanda said as Jack stepped up beside her and tapped at the bow on the papers.

"Insisted?" Jack laughed. "I can imagine. Who dealt with her?"

"I don't know," Amanda shrugged. "Mary, I guess. Our receptionist. I was out of the office. We all were. Except Mary. That happens. Not often. But this woman—Jill—came in and said she wanted you to have this. Everything was in order. Just wrap it in black lace and have me deliver it. She even provided the lace in a beautiful felt bag. Here, thank you."

She offered the bandana gingerly onto Jack's forearm. "Uh?"

Jack smiled tracing the edge of the black bow. "No, keep it, Ms. Pace. I have another in the Jeep."

Jack pulled the bow and took the top sheet from the bundle. He leaned over and held the paper to the beam from the headlight. He saw his name. His real name and a lawyer's name executing for The Tower Estate. Jack straightened and handed the sheet back to Amanda.

"So," he asked quietly, "did Mary say what this Jill person looked like?"

"No," Amanda shrugged dismissively. "I mean, it never came up. I mean, I don't even know if Mary spoke to the woman. I heard it was a woman. But, I'm sorry. I am feeling a little out of it. Anyway, we don't usually discuss what clients look like."

"Yes, of course not. You don't have to apologize. I'm out of it, too, I guess. Is…uh…is this…paper thing…uh…does it mean the tower is mine? That I'm being given the tower?"

"I'm here for just that reason," she smiled, then laughed and grabbed Jack by the elbow and whispered. "Well, we'll still have to confirm that you are the man named on this contract. You are, right? That's your name? I mean she gave us a picture and you sure look like the man in the photograph. This isn't one of those oogity-boogity impossibly ridiculous latex mask things is it? Some alien spy twilight limits thing?" She laughed again and impulsively hugged him, drawing back still laughing and gazing into his face as if he were an old, old friend.

Jack laughed with her, but he was distracted. "Photograph?" he asked when she caught her breath. The word had startled him. He'd never seen a camera anywhere near the Tower. "Do you have it with you?"

"I believe so. Why? Running out of souvenir glossies?"

"Right," he grinned, embarrassed, noticing how her face was even more beautiful when she laughed. "I don't need to see it. I think we're both happier when we're not in the professional mode, eh?"

She blanched. He had caught her off guard. She seemed afraid.

"I'm sorry," Jack said reaching to hold her hand.

She briskly walked past him toward the tower. She stopped at the porch and did not turn around. She pretended to look at the tower, eyeing it with a professional real estate gaze.

"No, you're right," she stated. "This is business. I don't know what came over me. Too…busy, I guess. Here." She reached into her inside breast pocket and pulled out a key. She discreetly bent and placed it on the top step. "That's your key. I'll send somebody from the agency to verify your identity."

Jack waited for her to turn around but she didn't. Instead she walked to the right, heading for the beach.

"Ms. Pace. Amanda," he called. "Wait."

She stopped at the edge of the light and turned. "Look," she said, her voice more tired than irritated though clearly she wanted distance between herself and Jack. "I've had a long day and we're done here and I'd like to go for a walk along the beach by myself. I'm sure you're a nice man and you'll have a lovely time here with your friend whenever she gets back. But I've no intention of playing at this."

Jack didn't move. He didn't say anything. He just stood and breathed and watched her. There was something about her. A sadness perhaps. Or perhaps the quality of her determination to deny her own vulnerability. It's true, he thought. People do fall in love with themselves, an idealized form of themselves. And that was okay, he decided. It was human. Tragic, maybe. Maybe he and she would almost succeed only to fail at the last moment. But the failure would not be love's loss, but love's proof of its transcendent power over death, a story that rang through the ages. If he were luckier, maybe his love would be a comedy and they would die in old age, only weeks apart, quietly in the home of a daughter on a Sunday morning. But it didn't matter. He was going to love, love his frailties, his strengths. He was even going to forgive himself when he hated his frailties and abused his strengths. He needed this world, this tower of mystery that he could not understand, that appeared and disappeared, shadow and light, in his confused and confusing life. There wasn't much he could do about it anyway.

He loved her already.

"Amanda, wait!" he called and ran up to her. "Didn't they tell you about this place? About the beach? You know, at night? How that line of trees is…well, not what it appears to be."

"What is this?" Amanda asked, biting her lower lip and nodding skeptically trying to find something, some way to shake the feeling that she was about to fall big. She had wanted to cry and now…what was it about this guy?

"Look," she continued, clearing her throat and shaking back some errant strands of hair, "maybe we ought to try this tomorrow."

"Did I tell you that I was a storyteller?" Jack cheerily asked, taking her by the arm and leading her back toward the tower. "Did you know the woman who owned this house was a teacher of fairy tales? And that she was probably a ghost? Yes, a ghost. But she made a fine cup of tea. I bet there's a cup in there with your name on it."

"A ghost? You've inherited a house from a ghost?"

"Most inheritances are from ghosts, aren't they?"

"Ha ha," she smirked, but with a glint in her eye. "You know what I mean."

"Well, I don't know for sure if she was a ghost. She might have been an angel or even a figment of my imagination. She might have been an alien. You saw that midnight movie thing, right?"

"Mister…," Amanda breathed out slowly.

"Call me, Jack. All my imaginary friends do."

"Fine, Jack. So you're a storyteller?"

Jack scooped up the key and slid it into the door lock. And he held it there.

The Man Who Longed for a Horse: Ironspike

The sun was just up. She had set the kettle on to boil. A bell rang once on the porch. Amanda opened the door. Nothing. The sky perfectly cloudless. Not a stirring even high in the trees. Her brow furrowed, but her lips offered a small smile. She stepped back to close the door when she noticed a flash of red on the mat. It was a red book. Her smile widened. She bent and picked up the book. A long black feather marked a page. She opened to the feather and began to read.

***

Once upon a time there was a man who longed for a horse. He was a crippled man whose legs had been broken in a war with the gods. In each hand he carried an iron spike which he plunged into the ground before him and then pulled himself forward on the flat of his belly. It was excruciating work but he managed to get where he was going through rain and snow and dry desert lands.

He dragged himself from place to place looking for food, for shelter, for something to do with his life. He often felt sorry for himself, but he never cried. He would accept handouts from those who stopped and had pity on him, but he never said thank you, nor did he even so much as look at the kind people who took the time to notice him. When he did get work he did it well, but he made no friends.

He never stayed long at a job because after a few weeks his mind would wander to images of wild horses galloping across a wide, grassy plain. In his vision he rode on the lead stallion laughing, naked and strong, riding into a rising sun. At the end of these reveries he would simply fall to the floor of whatever workshop he was in and begin digging into the floor dragging himself outside and on to the next town.

The crippled man traveled like this for years, growing ever more silent, ever more alone, taking less and less work. Occasionally he would hear of a stable job and drag himself to the gate of the farm and stare out into the fields. He would watch the horses, if any were out, but they always seemed too dull, too domesticated to hold the energy he knew he would release once he mounted his white stallion and rode into the sun. So he never got beyond the farm's gate. He would turn away and crawl on down the road to the next lonely town.

One day, as the man crawled toward another anonymous village, it began to rain. The man was not bothered by the downpour for he was accustomed to nature's elements pounding upon his back. He simply gritted his teeth and continued to crawl toward the village, but as he came to a bridge it began to rain harder and the rain turned to hail. The thunder and lightning sharply increased in intensity. The sky turned a pale green. The man knew what such a color meant and decided to wait out the storm under the bridge. He carefully pulled himself down the steep side of the river bed and nestled himself tightly between the bridge and the bank. After a while he fell asleep. Before long, however, he woke up with the waters of the river furiously lapping at his side.

The waters raged, spiked with broken trees, their branches twisted and lightning-scarred. A dead pig floated by and several drowned chickens. The man knew if he did not do something in the next few moments he, too, would be dead. He had never learned to swim. If he tried to float on the fast moving waters he knew the tree limbs would drag him and tumble him down to the bottom of the churning river. He winced in pain imagining his body gnawed by ravenous catfish and gar.

The man desperately began stabbing at the underside of the wooden bridge with his two iron spikes. His arms had become terribly strong pulling his body around the world. Swiftly he carved a hole in the bridge and pushed up a shattered plank. One more hand hold, he thought. It wouldn't take but two. Years of meager eating had kept him thin. He would easily be able to pull himself through the width of two bridge planks.

"One more and I'm safe," he said out loud. He stabbed frantically at the second plank.

"Yes!" he screamed as the plank gave way and he pushed his head through to the open air. He breathed deeply, hungrily into the pounding rain and hail. Then in a flash his breath was taken from him.

A rider on a dapple-grey horse was at the other end of the bridge galloping down hard upon him. Killed by a horse he thought in an instant of crushing disbelief. The man closed his eyes and did not even hear his own screaming. But the horse did not crush him. It reared when it saw his screaming, frightful head. The rider lost the reins and fell into the water, disappearing in a rolling tangle of uprooted brush. The horse stepped back, reared again, and it, too, slipped into the tumult and under the bridge, slamming into the man and pulling him into the flood.

Blind with fear and stunned by the deafening sounds of the tortured waters, the incessant thunder, and most vividly by the horrific screams of the panicked horse, the man slapped at the raging waters searching for something, anything to hold on to. Then something stabbed his back and he went down, his mouth opened in shock and the foaming waters rushed past his rotting teeth and filled his throat with foul-tasting death. Lost, he thought. That's all there is. All done, but good-bye. Good-bye, he thought, and this resolved him to his fate. He opened his eyes slowly, softly, to look upon whatever it would be that would take him away. He opened his eyes to look upon his killer and....

He popped back up to the surface. A reprieve, a reprieve. He screamed to the gods for help. No, no, he didn't want to die, and suddenly he felt something between his twisted legs. It was the horse. The horse! The gods had forgiven him and saved him with a horse! Sweet, sweet, gentle gods. His face relaxed for the first time in years. Tears came to his eyes and for the first time in his life his lips almost whispered the words, "Thank you."

And then he saw the blood in the water swirling out like a cloud, a mare's tail they called them, combs of white floating high in the heavens. But this cloud was red. In the man's thrashing he had plunged a spike into its throat again and again. The horse was dead. The softness left the man's face without a trace as he gripped his arms tighter around the horse's neck and blankly stared into the boiling black waters.

Several miles down stream the horse and its bitter rider drifted onto a sandy river bank. The man crawled off the bloated horse and vomited into the grass. He rolled over and propped himself on his elbows, stared at his strange savior as if upon a god fallen from the heavens. Fallen dead from the heavens. The tempest raged on for hours, but the man did not seek shelter. He lay there beside the horse through the night and the tears flowed freely from his dark and bloody eyes. Slowly, the storm lessened, the stars came out, but there was no moon. The man watched the stars fade to their own mysterious sleep as the day dawned clear and bright.

Birds began to fly about. He saw a few crows gathering beside a tangled knot of broken trees several yards further down stream. Amidst the debris he noticed an unnatural splash of color. He squinted, but could not discern what the patch of color could be. He pulled himself along the ground for a few feet and squinted again. It was the body of the ill-fated rider. Two crows hopped onto the body.

"No.... No!" the man screamed at the birds and threw one of his spikes. The crows flew off. The man crawled rapidly to the body. It was a young girl, maybe ten years old. He put his fist to his mouth and bit down hard. He could barely breathe. After a few moments he pulled the girl as gently as he could from her broken bough tomb. Then he just lay beside her gazing in a trance into the empty blueness of the sky thinking nothing, nothing at all. Minutes passed. The crows landed near them again and the man sat up and screamed and screamed and screamed. Then he covered his face with his hands and took one deep breath.

"Yes," he whispered and began crawling through the grass looking for the spike he had thrown at the crows. He found it and returned to the girl. Not looking at her face, he pulled her onto his back and began crawling toward the village. The crows circled above as he passed the horse. He didn't look back as he heard the birds land.

When the man got to the village on the other side of the bridge it was devastated. There had been a tornado and most of the homes and shops had been destroyed. Many people had been killed. Several children ran up to the man as he crawled into the outskirts of the village. They didn't say anything to him, but ran back toward a group of men who stood in what remained of the village square. A few moments later the men gathered around the man staring at him. A red-haired man said a name, but the crippled man didn't catch what it was. Then another man took the body of the girl from the man's back. The redhead asked him what happened. The man told the villager there had been a flash flood and the girl had been washed into the river. Another man asked about the horse the girl had been riding and he was told it had been drowned, too.

The crippled man said he felt very sorry for the girl and the village and asked if he could be permitted to help them rebuild their homes and shops.

He told the villagers he was very strong though he could not walk and that he was very good with a hammer. They told him they could not pay, but he said all he needed was a little bread and water. Then the villagers were silent for a moment before they turned from the man and formed a whispering circle. Occasionally one of the men would toss a glance over a shoulder and scowl.

They did not like the feel of this dirty man with his mud-encrusted hair, flies thick around his head. His legs were little more than blackened stubs, the colorless rags on his body barely kept him decent. He was a terribly ugly man and there was something in the man's voice, something in the way he would not look at them. There was something about the man's story they did not trust. The man looked up at them just once during this whispered council. Seeing their suspicions, their disgust, he quickly looked away and began to crawl back the way he had come.

A woman suddenly rode up on a black stallion and jumped to the ground. She ran to the villager who was still holding the body of the child. She wrenched the girl from his hands and fell sobbing to the muddy earth, the girl pressed tightly to her breast. After a few minutes the woman looked up and asked what had happened to her girl. The men nodded to the crippled man who had stopped when the woman rode up but was now crawling away again. The woman called after him and he slowly turned and sat up.

"What happened, sir?" the woman asked, tears still streaming from her green eyes. "How did you find her? How did you bring her back here?"

The man told her what he had told the villagers. Though he knew he should be respectful to this woman, he dared not look at her for he could feel the hot shame rising in his face. But she did not say anything. She did not take offense at his disgrace. She stood with the girl in her arms and walked to him and stretched out her hand.

"Thank you," she said. "Thank you for bringing her back to me."

"It's the least I could do, ma'am," the man said and he hurriedly turned and started to crawl away.

"Horace," the woman called to one of the villagers. "Is Sol still in the blacksmith's? Yes? Well, bring him. Bring him now." She turned back to the crippled man. "Sir, wait. I must thank you. I want to give you a gift."

The man could not speak. Tears welled in his eyes as he looked into the woman's face. He knew. He knew. Horace, the redhead, trotted up with a saddled white stallion at his side.

"I...can...not...accept it," the man stuttered. "I...do...not...deserve it."

"You deserve it," the woman answered. "It is the least I can do. Horace. Will." The woman gestured for the men to pick up the crippled man and place him on the horse.

"No…no," the man protested weakly as they lifted him onto the back of the white stallion. "No…no," but then his body touched the bow of the saddle and his spikes fell from his hands. They fell from his hands and turned in mid-air into golden birds who circled above the village calling a song that sounded like golden hammers on silvered water. Instantly all the homes and shops were restored, but restored in gold and silver and precious jewels beyond measure. Then the golden birds flew down to rest so tenderly upon the little girl's breast and their song changed so sweetly, so smoothly. It sounded like apples touching clouds, like honey tasting midnight. The girl opened her eyes and softly she called her mother's name.

The man on the horse was shining, naked. His skin had turned from a grimy black to a glistening white and gold. His hair sparkled clean and long with beautiful, elegant curls. His legs were no longer useless weights. They were strong, young; his calf and thigh muscles flexed brilliantly. He raised his eyes to look into the noon day sun, spurred the horse once with his firm, narrow heels, and rose into the sky laughing with a joy that still rings in that village to this very day. For the man came back from his ride to the sun. He married the woman. They raised horses together which were renowned throughout the land for their beauty and gentleness. Best of all, they had many fine children and grandchildren who all lived happily to a ripe old age.

The man who longed for a horse had found a home.